[illegible] BLISS

FORMERLY GAME ENDER

BJ HARVEY

Seeking Bliss

Originally published as Game Ender

Edited by Elle at Love N Ink
Cover Designed by BJ Harvey
Photo sourced from Shutterstock

ISBN: Epub - 978-0-473-37458-7
ISBN: Mobi - 978-0-473-37459-4
ISBN: Print - 978-0-6455196-5-5

Created with Vellum

COMPLETE BLISS SERIES READING ORDER

Temporary Bliss (Bliss #1)—Mac and Daniel

True Bliss (Bliss #2)—Kate and Zander

Reclaiming Bliss (Bliss #3)—Sean and Sam

formerly Blissful Surrender

Permanent Bliss (Bliss #4)—

Mac & Daniel's Wedding

Finding Bliss (Bliss #5)—Noah and Zoe

Building Bliss (formerly Game Player)—Matt and Mia

Secret Bliss (formerly Game Maker)

—Zack and Danika

Faking Bliss (formerly Game Saver)

—Cade and Abi

Seeking Bliss (formerly Game Ender)

—Thomas and Amy

Promising Bliss (formerly Game Breaker)

—Cameron and Sarah

Beautiful Bliss (formerly Game Planner)

—Jase and Natalie

DEDICATION

To A & A, Chicken and Rice for life

PROLOGUE

Thomas

There are certain things that are guaranteed to get any man—macho or not—to the doctor. Anything wrong with appendages located in the very important area between the hips down to mid-thigh will always warrant immediate action.

The slight burning sensation from my morning leak that turned into a stream of fire by mid-afternoon *definitely* fell into that category so with a call to my best friend Cade, I leave the office, telling my secretary that I had an urgent meeting come up and would be gone for the rest of the day.

A short drive later, I quickly make my way into the ER of Northwestern Hospital where Cade works as a doctor, and walked to the reception desk.

"I'm here to see Cade Carsen."

"Sir, you'll need to fill out this form and take a seat," the receptionist says, holding out a clipboard to me.

"You don't understand," I reply, my heart rate spiking as I take a quick cursory glance at the filled chairs behind me, the air becoming stifling with bacteria and germs that I swear are launching an attack on my immune system with every breath I take. I turn my attention back to the now scowling—actually downright scary—desk clerk. "Cade's my roommate, best friend actually. Can you please page him? He's expecting me."

She scrutinizes me, her eyes scanning down my body and back up again.

"Riiiiight," she replies skeptically, like every second person tries that excuse to avoid exposure to the waiting room petri dish.

"Thomas?" the most welcome voice in the world says, using my nickname that only a select few use. I turn around to see the wife of another of my best friends, Mac, standing beside me, an orange Chicago Bears hoodie covering up her scrubs. "Everything okay?"

I release a huge sigh of relief, my future health and life expectancy thanking the heavens for this serendipitous stroke of luck.

"Hey, I'm here to see Cade. He's expecting me but the *lovely* desk clerk here has obviously heard this story a million times and doesn't believe me."

She bursts out laughing before turning toward the desk and leaning over it. "Hey Nancy, I can vouch for this miscreant. I can take him through to Dr. Carsen."

Nancy eyes me suspiciously, pursing her thin lips as she looks me up and down then nods her permission to Mac. *What am I, chopped fucking liver?*

"Have a nice day, *Nancy,*" I say with a saccharine sweet smile on my face, knowing that I probably shouldn't come here if I ever need emergency medical attention.

Mac giggles beside me, making tut-tut sounds and drawing my attention.

"What?" I ask innocently.

She smirks at me. "You know what, Mr. Charming."

"Obviously didn't work with *Nancy.*"

"Nancy is just used to people's bullshit. She sees people like you trying to cut in line every day, all day."

"I wasn't trying to—" She snorts and quirks a brow at me, it's such a 'mom' look that I can't help but grin down at her as she swipes the ID card hanging off her neck across a keypad, gaining access through to the ER and leading me through the double doors.

"Does that work on Danny boy?" I ask, betting everything I own that it does.

"Why do you think he's always smiling?" she says and it's then I want to high five my friend Daniel for finding—and nailing down permanently—the woman beside me.

"So why are you braving the ER center when you could just see Cade tonight at Poker?"

I falter—just for a second—and eagle-eye Mac doesn't miss it. We come to a stop outside a door labeled 'Doctors' Lounge' and she turns to face me. "Is this a professional visit? You can tell me, I can't tell anyone. Call it patient—sexy nurse confidentiality," she says with a wink.

I look her up and down and shake my head with a grin playing on my lips. "Sorry, love, unless I get the full naughty nurse treatment, short dress, garters, stockings and heels, no deal."

She pouts and play punches me. "Sorry, bruiser. Only superheroes get that kind of special treatment."

"I've got some latent super powers. They're activated when you—"

"Thomas," Cade says, his voice an amused warning as he

comes to a stop in front of us. "Are you coming on to the nurses again?"

"Unfortunately for us, we missed the boat with this one. She's well and truly off the market."

Cade snorts. "You'd hope so considering she married Dan how many years ago now?"

"Five? No wait . . ." Mac holds out her hand, biting her lip as she counts her fingers. "Oh, I don't know, a *while.*"

We all laugh at that, Mac's cheeks going uncharacteristically pink.

"I think Dan must be losing his touch if you can't remember *those* kind of details."

"Or else the three kidlets are *stopping* any kind of touching at all," I retort.

"On that note, I'll love and leave you," Mac announces, leaning forward and giving us both a kiss on the cheek before waving and walking away.

"Shall we?" Cade asks, sweeping an arm toward the short corridor.

"Lead the way."

"So . . . what's the emergency?" He says as soon as the consultation room door closes behind us.

I turn toward him, my heart pounding in my chest. But this is Cade, my best friend. He's probably seen and heard it all. I know for a fact he's seen more blood and gore than anyone should ever see.

Struggling to find the words, I take a slow, calming deep breath.

This is my trip on the downtown inferno train. It's not like I've ever gone through something like this before, and I hope to Christ I never have to go through it again.

"First, you've gotta swear on your life that you will not breathe a word of this to anyone."

His lips twitch and he lifts an eyebrow at me. "So it involves your dick then?"

My eyes widen, fuck knows why. It's not like it *wouldn't* be my junk and I know it *is* my junk, but for some reason, hearing him say it like that irks me.

"What makes you say that?" I ask like an idiot considering I called him just an hour ago and told him I was coming to see him and needed his professional opinion. All that aside, he's going to need to know that my problem is with my most prized body part in order to give me whatever pills, injections, or bleach treatment required,.

"I think I've caught something."

"Something?"

"An STD." And just like that Cade's amused look vanishes in an instant and it's in this moment that I love the man because he's suddenly all business.

Most other guys would take the opportunity to rib me about the correct use of condoms or—if it were Matt Taylor, one of my best friend's brothers—tell me to do a damn scratch and sniff test next time.

Man hands go to my belt and I start to unzip my fly.

"Wait!" he says quickly. "Before you flop it out and show me *far* too much of yourself. What are your symptoms?"

My hands still and my eyes back up to his. "Ah . . ."

"Thomas, I can't treat you unless I know what we're looking at."

"It burns when I . . ." Fuck, why am I suddenly embarrassed about this shit. *Because it's fucking mortifying.* I clear my throat. "It burns when I take a piss and there's this weird *stuff* coming out—"

"Right," he says quickly. "Now we're getting somewhere. When did you first notice that something was wrong?" He tilts his head toward the hospital bed and I move that way, undoing my pants before sitting down on the gurney.

"Maybe a week ago. It was just a niggle, like something wasn't right but I went to the men's room at lunch and knew something was wrong. So here I am."

"Good decision," he says, walking over to stand beside the bed, leaning over to pull some gloves from the dispenser on the wall. "Show me the problem."

He doesn't show anything other than a perfect bedside manner as I pull down my underwear and show him my dick. *Things you never imagine having to show your best friend, check.*

"You've got a sexually transmitted infection. I'll need a urine sample to confirm, though," he announces matter-of-factly and having finished examining my junk, steps back and pulls off the offending rubber gloves.

"Can't you just give me a shot?"

His responding snort is the only crack in his professional demeanor.

"I'm doing a full screen for STDs and you're honestly thinking that I can clear it up with a *shot?*" He's right of course, but seriously, why hasn't someone invented that already?

Burning sensation when you pee? Have a shot of 'VD-be-gone.'

Weird 'stuff' coming out of places it shouldn't? Bend over and one little prick will clear it right up.

"Will it go back to normal?" I ask irrationally, knowing it's an STD and not castration but a man can never be too sure of these things. I've watched those *Sex Sent Me to the ER* programs, I know that weird things can happen.

He chuckles and smirks. "Yes, Thomas. You'll lose the STD tag but the drugs won't make it any bigger." *Fucking smart ass.*

"Thanks. I think I'm covered in that department, Carsen."

"So the Swedish Cock Pump I found in the guest room must've been yours."

"You're hilarious. If this doctor thing doesn't work out, you should think about stand up."

"I'll take that under advisement."

"Seriously though?" I ask, all humor gone for the moment.

He steps forward and claps me on the arm. "Finish the antibiotics I'm going to prescribe you, and once we know what you're dealing with, you'll just need to come back in and get retested in three months. And if I were you, I'd sit down and make a list of everyone who even looked at your cock recently."

"How recent?"

"It can't be that big a list, surely?"

My silence speaks volumes—to the both of us—and the fact that I even have to think about it is a blinding smack in the face.

"You also can't have sex until you're clear. Public health and all that," Cade says flippantly.

"Even a party for one?" I ask, partly joking but seriously hoping he's not going to rule out Mrs. Palmer fun.

He struggles to hold back a grin. "You can't infect your

hand—or the penis pump—so you're fine. But maybe this can be a lesson to you."

"To wrap it before I slap it?" He winces and I swear his thighs tense on autopilot.

"Can't believe you *didn't*. Safe Sex 101."

"It was just once . . ."

"Well at least you know when you got it . . . right?" he says with an obvious sound of relief.

I suddenly feel embarrassed about my recent Laissez-faire approach to sex and women. "One girl I've seen twice, a few months apart . . ."

"Thomas . . ." he growls. "Both times without protection?"

I nod, feeling his recrimination deep in my bones. "So I'm guessing I need to tell the women in between now?"

"That's my professional instruction, yes." Shit. That might be a long-ish list considering there were three months in between visits with said 'one-time thing.'

"Ever thought of keeping it in your pants for a while?" he says ironically, considering he's been my wingman more times than I've had hot dinners.

"The last time I did that was when I was a teenager."

"And look where you are now. I'm so proud," he says, wiping a fake tear away. This is no longer my doctor speaking, this is my best friend of fifteen years.

"Says the man who's now getting it regularly from his former mother-buffer friend with benefits."

"Who I wasted ten months not being with because I thought it *was* just a one-time thing," he retorts. "And I would give up everything to make up that time now that I know what I've got with Abi." Cade and Abi got together a year ago then again a few months ago. Now that they're together–as in full relationship with a *lot* of benefits that I have to hear *far* too regularly–I can't imagine them ever *not* being together. They're just that perfect for one another.

"I just haven't found the right woman. You snatched her off the market before I could even introduce myself," I tease.

"You're a funny guy."

"A funny guy with an STD."

"Let's see what the tests come back with and we'll go from there."

"That's it. I'm never having sex again." I reach down and gently cup my crotch. "It's okay buddy, we'll get you all fixed up and happy again."

Cade quirks a brow at me, his expression one of 'what the fuck are you doing?' "You need a girl–no, a *woman*–to knock you on your ass and make you want to change your ways."

"Like there's even a woman out there who'd *ever* make me want to do that."

"Prove it."

"What?"

"Prove it. No more casual sex, definitely no un*safe* sex, and hold out for the right woman."

I don't answer straight away, giving his suggestion the respect it deserves, because what harm can it do. Right now, sex is so far from my mind, what harm is a little abstinence going to cause?

"Care to make it worth my while?"

He barks out a laugh, shaking his head at me. "Only you would bet on your sex life."

I shoot him a grin. "What can I say, I value the future happiness of my cock very highly."

"Obviously," he muses. "I bet you can't hold out."

"Why would I?"

"Just try it. You might surprise yourself."

"You don't think I can do it, do you?" I ask, not sure how I'm feeling about the lack of faith Cade has in me.

"Nope. I give it a month, or the first hot redhead to look your way. Whatever comes first."

"The woman *always* comes first, Doctor Carsen. Have I taught you nothing?"

He steps toward me and holds his arm out. "I bet you can't hold out."

I grasp hold of his hand, looking him dead straight in the eye. "I'm telling you, the next woman I take to bed will be the *one*."

His head jerks back and his eyes grow wide. "That's a big call, Caldwell."

"I'm sick of fucking around. Look where and *what* it got me."

"So abstinence makes the heart grow fonder?" he asks, a smile playing on his lips.

"Or the cock grow harder."

"Probably both," he says, full out grinning now. "You sure about this?"

"Yep." The more I think about it, the surer I actually am. If I've learned anything from this, it's that it's high time I had a mid-thirties life overhaul.

With the decision made, it's then that I make my vow to Cade.

"I swear to you, on our friendship and my future happiness, the next woman that gets me, will be the one that gets me and *only* me."

And blue balls and wet dreams be damned, I'm going to

damn well stick to it.

Amy

Two weeks later

Drama in the club where I work is not uncommon. Jealous girlfriends, testosterone and alcohol-fueled scuffles between guys looking for some action, I've seen it all.

But this was different. Thomas Caldwell–the man I've admired from afar but would never go for–sitting on a stool at the bar next to a rather unexpected woman and she was shrieking at him.

He frowns, the fingers of one hand gripping a bottle of Coors on the bar in front of him, his arm draped over the back of the obviously irate woman's chair.

"Michelle, I'm not saying—"

"You just told me your man-whore dick is infected—"

"*Was,* it's not anymore. Can you keep your voice down?" he says, his expression resigned and–if I'm not mistaken–he almost looks embarrassed. Totally not his normal demeanor.

"And that I should get tested," she continues.

"Yes," he replies, dropping his head—and his hand—and taking a long pull from his beer.

"Asshole!" she shrieks–*again*–standing up and throwing her gin and tonic at his face leaving him wide-eyed and drenched.

I stand there equal parts shock and amused, watching in avid fascination as she grabs her purse and storms out of the bar.

Thomas doesn't move, frozen in place as he watches his disgruntled—okay furious—date leave the building.

Looking back to his beer, his shoulders sag, and his eyes glued to his beer bottle and part of me braces for what he might do next.

But he doesn't do anything. He grabs a napkin and wipes his face then just sits there, staring into space, his body language screaming defeat, the cocky asshole I've come to expect nowhere to be seen.

Feeling the need to do something, so I put the cocktail glass I'm polishing down behind the bar and make my way toward him.

Looking up, he lifts his chin in my direction before returning to the seemingly focused examination of his drink, his fingers picking mindlessly at the paper label.

"All good, Thomas?" I ask cheerfully. Normally I'd relish in such a scene where a man's chickens come home to roost. I'm not a prude. Hell, my two best friends have made sure of that with all their sex stories and exploits. But something about his body language, so different from his normal confident self, stops me from being a snarky 'I told you so' bitch.

"Nope," he replies, eyes meeting mine. *Despondent, thy name is Thomas.*

"Want another beer?"

"Yep." He doesn't look away. He just sits there, elbows resting on the bar, hands holding a now empty bottle, gaze glued to mine.

I turn around and bend down to the fridge behind the bar, pulling out another Coors and returning to Thomas, handing over the new drink and tugging at the empty bottle in front of him.

"Want to talk about it?" His eyes flash but as quick as it appears, it's gone, and like a light has been switched, his edible full lips twitch and slowly curl up into a grin.

"You going to be my shrink *and* serve me drinks, Amy? Because I don't need a therapist but I *do* need a never-ending supply of alcohol."

"But I thought lending an ear was part of the job description?"

"So you offer extra services too?" he replies snottily.

"You're sounding rather defensive there, Thomas. And to be honest, you're being a bit of a dick when all I'm trying to do is help."

"Not at all, blue eyes," he retorts with a cheesy—and cocky—smile, made worse when he adds an unnecessary and rather exaggerated wink. I fully admit it makes my belly flutter but I don't dare let him know that.

Instead I place my hands on my hips and lift my brow. "I know your type, Thomas Caldwell. You're good looking and cocky with a walk that tells women you know what you've got in your pants and you definitely know how to use it. I bet if I was anyone else, you'd probably say something along the lines of 'did it hurt when you fell from heaven?' Am I close?"

"You're not anyone else. You're Amy."

"What does that mean?" I ask, the hair on the back of my neck prickling with awareness.

He shrugs and lifts his beer to his mouth, eyes pinned to mine as he takes a long sip. My gaze drops to his throat, the slow measured movements of his Adam's apple suddenly fascinating.

I've always appreciated Thomas. His charm, his beautiful tousled blond hair, his crisp sea-blue eyes and most assuredly his body made for sin.

From the first time I saw him at the club, I wanted him and for more than just an orgasm. But the more I watched him, the more I discovered that one night of assuredly good sex was all he was willing to give anyone—maybe everyone—and I didn't want to open myself up to the world of hurt that a man like Thomas would certainly deliver had I let my vagina get her way.

So I've admired from afar, tortured myself with night after night of watching him seduce women with a wink, a smile and sweet—but most assuredly dirty—words whispered in their ears. I can't say it hasn't been entertaining though.

Now though, I'm curious over the dramatic departure of his date and not being the type of woman to ever let something like that go, I don't stop myself from addressing the elephant in the room.

"So your date . . ."

"Not a date," he replies gruffly. "A woman I slept with a few months ago."

"Ah," I reply. "She wasn't happy that you're a one-night wonder?"

He chokes, spluttering as his wide eyes bore into me, his mouth agape. "What makes you say that?" His tone is cautious, almost intrigued.

I lean into the bar, inadvertently bringing my face closer to his. "I've been working this bar for five years and you've been coming in here for at least a few of those," I explain, grabbing a cloth and wiping down the bar in front of him. "I've seen it all. I've seen most of you guys come in here on the prowl and leave with more than your fair share of willing prey."

"Prey, huh?"

I grin at him. "Well, maybe that's a *bit* of a stretch, but you can't tell me you haven't spread the love far and wide over the years. Even still, I've never seen you get a drink to the face before."

"She was pissed at me."

"You don't say." My sarcasm isn't subtle and he definitely doesn't miss it.

"I've narrowed it down to five reasons why a woman would throw a drink at a man."

He leans back and crosses his perfectly toned arms over his chest.

"Impart your wisdom, oh wise bartender." He takes another drink of his beer and—yet again—watching me like a hawk. *I wish he'd stop watching me.*

My confidence wavers under his intense stare but when I catch a knowing glint in his eye, it riles me up. There's nothing worse than a guy who hides his unease behind a cocky façade, *especially* when I know there's something genuine hiding there.

It's one of the worst qualities a guy can have. It's disingenuous and fake and if there's two things I hate—in anyone—it's that.

I square my shoulders and stand up straight, deciding to let him have it, putting my hands out in front of me to count on my fingers.

"One, you cheated on her." He shakes his head, an amused smile playing on his lips.

"Nope. Next."

"Two, connected to the first, you hooked up with her sister, best friend or mother . . ." He snorts at that one, chuckling under his breath as he shakes his head again.

"Right, then, the last three," I continue. "Three through five are offending her family/job/friends or outfit, asking her to pay for your date and lastly, giving her an STD."

His eyes grow wide and he sits bolt upright.

Bingo.

"Who told you?"

"What?"

"Did you overhear me talking to Michelle?"

"Oh my God," I say before I can filter, taking a step back.

"It's nothing. Well it was something, but now it's treated so it's a non-issue. I just have to . . ." he reaches up and grips the back of his neck, his head dropped down toward the ground.

Gone is the facade, this is the real man underneath it all. The one I've heard about but never seen. "I have to inform women I've been with in case I've given it to them."

"Thomas, I didn't know. I was just guessing."

"Shit. If this wasn't bad enough already."

"Thomas, it happens—"

"Oh believe me, I'm well aware of that. I've had the test and taken the antibiotics to prove it," he says bitterly.

"So that's why she stormed out of here like her ass was on fire?"

"That'll be why," he replies sarcastically.

"I'm not going to tell anyone," I reply, needing to reassure him, somehow make him feel a little bit better.

He sighs loudly, I'm guessing part relief part resignation. "It's fine. She was the last one. I figured that by meeting her in a public place I might avoid a scene."

"Yeah, sorry to tell you but any high maintenance woman like that will *always* make a scene when given news like that. My guess is she wasn't happy with the one-night stand part of the arrangement so she was probably already feeling pretty stabby when it came to the subject of you. Telling her you *might* have also given her the Clap looked like it was the last straw."

"It wasn't the Clap," he mutters.

"Sorry?"

"It wasn't gonorrhea, it was chlamydia."

"Right. The Clam then," I reply cheerfully and finally I break through, a wry grin making an appearance.

Noticing his beer is nearly empty, I nod to the bottle. He pours the rest into his mouth and hands me the empty. "Thanks. You didn't have to be nice about this."

"I'm not exactly going to sell drinks being a bitch, am I?"

He chuckles and I take just a moment—just a smidge—to admire the beauty that is Thomas Caldwell, smiling and relaxed after what must've been a difficult conversation with the long gone Michelle.

I freely admit that Thomas is hot and he's featured in my bean-flicking highlight reel more than once.

Would I ever tell him or *anybody* that fact? Not on your life, Nelly.

But I'm glad I've been able to make him smile, everyone deserves that after a shitty day.

One thing is for sure, I know that underneath that cocky, sex on legs, 'want him to bend me over and do me nasty' exterior, there's also a decent human being who is more than the 'love 'em and leave 'em' façade he's known for. Beyond my already high on the Richter scale physical attraction to him, it's a definite blow considering the way he's been with me today.

Because after a discussion like this, I know I've been instantly relegated from a potential bedmate to forever being his friend's best friend and nothing more because everyone knows that guys think with their dicks first and their minds later.

I'm simply a convenient ear in the right place at the right time. Unfortunately for me, it's the *wrong* time for Thomas to see me as anything else either.

I've been friend-zoned by circumstance and by an STD of all things. There's one for the history books.

1

Amy

Baby showers. They're both awesome and torturous.

We've played games, gorged on baby-themed, pregnant-woman-friendly snacks, all the while carrying out the well-practiced 'smile and nod' gesture whenever someone mentions how big my stomach is, how happy I must be, and finally how the 'pregnancy glow' looks good on me.

There have been discussions about baby names, the sharing of birth stories, and the imparting of well-meaning wisdom about what I should do when my son is finally born.

Don't get me wrong, I'm over the moon that I'm going to be meeting my baby boy in four weeks' time. I'm excited about being a mom, but I've never been the happy, clappy socialite who talks about these things.

As you can imagine, the last seven months have been anything but uneventful.

It's been one of those periods of time where decisions made in an instant—albeit drunken ones—have changed the course of my future, given that I'm sitting on a chair in the middle of *my* baby shower.

That's not to say that I regret the previously unseen detour I've taken, more self-imposed contemplation and being slapped in the face with my actions and the resulting consequences.

I've always been an over-thinker; a typical girl who fixates, analyzes—and overanalyzes—experiences, interactions, and problems as they arise before acting or reacting.

The first life-altering decision I made was accepting an invitation for after work drinks with a co-worker.

Cue three weeks later and that denial that every woman has had at least sometime in their lives when that monthly curse us women face decides to go M.I.A.

A myriad of reasons went through my head for that welcome—yet not always fun—visitor's absence. Was it stress, was it because of that green tea and kale detox I tried—and failed with—last month? Was the moon in retrograde with Uranus screwing up everyone's period? Or was it because those after work drinks that led to good (not great) sex were destined to have a longer-lasting effect than the hangover and regrets I woke up with the next morning?

One week later, I bit the bullet and drove twenty minutes out of the way to buy an over the counter pregnancy test from a CVS where nobody would recognize me.

Three positive tests later and I was curled up on the floor of my apartment in a blubbering mess.

I'm what I'd call the strong silent observant type, with a razor sharp tongue when required, staunchly independent, but loyal to a fault. My two closest friends—Mia and Abi—are the only ones in my inner circle and along with my dad and stepmom. They're my 'home.'

So in my time of need, it was those four people I turned to and it's been those four people–who've had my back. They've been the ones holding my hand through the ultrasounds, the OB/GYN appointments, and in Mia's case, sitting at my back during Lamaze class.

All of them are people who I don't ever want to be without and hope I'll never have to be.

They've all pushed their way through my defenses. When the father of my baby—let's call him the sperm donor—told me that he would have absolutely nothing to do with me or our child. It was Abi and Mia who had my back, battling the overwhelming urge to hunt him down and fuck him up, or castrate him, which I must admit I had to think about for a minute (or ten).

See, the father of my baby boy is not a stranger, because I honestly think that would've been a hell of a lot easier. No, the epic part of my decision eight months ago was to share a drink or five with a co-worker when the club was closed. I fell for his cocky grin, charming words, and listened to my traitorous vagina, having the clichéd one-night stand on the bar top of Throb.

He wasn't the cocky grin and charming words I wanted though. I couldn't have the one I wanted so—as bad as it sounds—I took what I thought at the time was the next best temporary thing.

Here I am now, almost nine months pregnant with a large belly, cankles, a 'pregnancy glow' which includes chubby cheeks and adult acne, boobs out to there and I honestly can't remember what my lady parts look like any more, let alone *want* to know, even if they could be found without the need for a weed whacker. And I'm confronted with the reality of very soon becoming a single mom.

"So Amy," Mia's mom Helen says, drawing everyone's attention. "Are you looking forward to the birth?"

Mia and I met five years ago when she was visiting Chicago to see her brother.

I'd just started at Throb and was the new bartender on the block, figuratively of course. It was only my second week and I was still fucking up on an hourly—okay maybe half daily—basis.

All Mia had to do was giggle at my attempt to make her Long Island Iced Tea and we were bonded for life.

I met my other best friend Abi at yoga class a few years ago. She had just transitioned into a downward facing dog pose when she accidentally farted then giggled about it. She did a quick sneak peek around the room to see if anyone else had heard it and when she met my eyes, we both burst out laughing, collapsing on the floor. We've been close ever since.

The fact that Abi is married to Cade who is best friends with Noah—Mia's sister Zoe's husband—and Mia is now married and babied to Noah's brother Matt. It's like three degrees of separation instead of six with this group but it totally works.

I shoot Helen a fifty percent fake/fifty percent genuine smile. The sincere part of it being because she's Helen, my second mom who pretty much adopted me the first time Mia took me home to Indiana to meet her.

"Not the birth, but definitely meeting my son," I reply, rubbing my stomach affectionately. "He may think my bladder is his personal trampoline and he doesn't like letting me sleep right now, but I'm ready. I think I am anyway."

Abi looks at me and grins. "I'm *definitely* looking forward to it. It's time to meet my godson."

Mia's head snaps to Abi. "*Your* godson? Um, hello? What am I? Chopped liver?"

I shudder at the thought of liver. Organs are gross, doesn't matter how you cook them, hide them, or dress them up. They're still organs and it's just eww.

"Girls . . ." Helen warns, her 'don't test me' tone cutting through the room.

I snigger at both Helen and my two friends.

Another friend of the group, Mac, wades in. "Can I just add, as a woman with *three* kids, they've all got multiple godparents. In fact," she looks to the women in the room then out to the kitchen and dining area where all the guys have congregated. "Most of the people here are connected to at least one if not all of my children."

"That's just so you have babysitters on tap," her friend Kate jibes. Kate is Mia's sister-in-law and Mac's best friend. I don't think I'll ever get over how incestuous this group is.

"No!" Mac replies with a wry grin. We all look at her and she bursts out laughing.

"Okay, maybe. Just a little. My point is that you can have as many godparents or significant adult role models in your son's life as you want. There's no limit."

"Deal!" Mia announces, poking her tongue out at Abi and all I can do is shake my head and grin at them.

"Boys," Mac hollers. "It's time for cake."

"Got it," her husband Daniel shouts back and I smile

because, at the end of the day, it's cake. If something is wrong? Cake. If you're PMSing? Cake again.

If you're pregnant at a baby shower with all these happy couples and it unintentionally smacks you in the face with the fact that you're eighteen months pregnant–okay almost thirty-six weeks–and you don't have a loving partner at your back, at least there's cake.

So basically, it's all about the cake.

Then Daniel and the rest of the male contingent walk into the room with Thomas walking in behind them, looking all hot and sexy. My heart sighs, the butterflies in my stomach start fluttering, and my lady parts that have been long forgotten about indicate their interest in reincarnation.

I did think it was weird when I saw he was at my baby shower but then again, all of the husbands came along so I figured he was just a ring-in or had nothing better to do.

When I look away to distract myself from him, I see all these people who chose to come to my shower today and it hits me how many people are here and the fact that they're actually here for me. Not because they are friends of friends, but for me, and just like that I'm the loony emo pregnant lady again.

"Aww," all of the women say. When they see all of their guys standing next to their significant others—bar Thomas of course—I lose it, burying my face in my hands to hide the tears falling down my cheeks.

"Amz, it's okay," Abi says. I can't see her face but her hands on my legs tell me she's kneeling on the floor in front of me.

I wipe my eyes and look up at her. "I'm fine," I reply quietly, my voice cracking. I quickly clear my throat when she gives my hand a squeeze. "Honestly, I'm okay." I glance around the room. "You guys are all just ridiculously good looking."

That earns me chuckles and grins, and thankfully, the 'oh poor Amy' mood in the room is broken.

Half an hour later, I hoist myself out of the recliner chair for a bathroom break. On my way back through the kitchen, I see Cade at the island in the middle of the room making drinks.

"Hey," I say, stopping on the opposite side of the counter from him.

"Hey. Are you doing okay? You look tired," he says, and I roll my eyes.

"You're off duty today, Doctor Carsen."

He shrugs and grins at me. "It's just habit now."

"Do I need to tell Abi that her husband needs another holiday?"

"We only just got back from our honeymoon," he says with a laugh.

"Overworked and undersexed then, your *wife* needs to up her game."

"If she upped her game anymore I wouldn't be *able* to work."

"TMI, dude. That is more than I need to know about you two."

He just grins at me and finishes what he's doing, but instead of grabbing the glasses and moving back to the living room, he leans on the counter and watches me.

"I saw you watching Thomas, you know." I freeze in place, wondering what the hell I'm supposed to do now.

"I was watching everyone," I reply, hedging my bets and hoping he'll change topics.

"He's a good guy, but . . ." he stops and narrows his brows

but he's piqued my interest now. I need to know what he was going to say. You can never end a sentence in but and *not* finish it. It's the law, or some rule, surely?

"But what?" I say urgently like my next breath is reliant on hearing the end of his sentence.

Cade doesn't call me out. He just looks over my shoulder for a minute then back to me. "I love him like a brother but he's lost. He's had a *lot* of changes happen in his life recently and I don't think, I mean, I don't *know* that he would be the type of guy you need right now."

"What? I don't . . . I'm not . . ." I stutter my words before taking a deep breath and composing my shocked self. "Given my current *condition,* the last thing I would ever be looking for is a man. Is he good looking? Yes. Do I think he'd be good for some fun? Of course. Am I looking for some fun right now? Hell no. Look at what happened last time I let loose in *that* department."

By the time I finish my little over-zealous explanation, Cade is grinning at me. "God, you're just like Abi."

"Except for the wife bit?"

"Yes, there is that," he replies. "Have you heard from 'he who shall not be named'?"

"You mean the 'sperm donor,'" I say, complete with air quotations.

"Yes, the poor excuse for a man."

"Oh don't call him a man, that's being *way* too generous," I reply sarcastically. "And in answer to your question, no I haven't, and I honestly don't expect to. I did my duty and told him I was pregnant. He made it *very* clear that he wanted no part in it and would prefer if I 'took care of it.' As far as I'm concerned we're all better off without him. It's good that he took off when he did." I rub my tummy, my protective instinct kicking in at the mere mention of the baby daddy.

"We're all here for you, Amz. Now and always," he says, moving around the island and hooking an arm around my shoulder.

"Does this mean our well-meaning chat is over?" I tease. "And would you like some help carrying the drinks?"

"I think you're carrying enough already, Amz. You go ahead and I'll be right behind you."

The Friday night after the baby shower, I'm pottering around behind the upstairs bar when Sean walks down the corridor and stops opposite me.

"Amy, why are you still here? You were supposed to leave an hour ago," he says, leaning his hands on the wooden top. If he wasn't my boss and I didn't know him as well as I do, I'd totally think the whole black shirt, black pants, commanding look was hot. But because it's Sean, he doesn't have any effect on me.

"Jessie was run off her feet so I thought I'd just help her out," I reply honestly.

"It's supposed to be your last day and I sent you home because you are exhausted."

"It's fine," I say, waving him off.

"Amy," he growls under his breath. "It's not busy anymore so you can now go home and put your feet up like the doctor told you to do."

"I was just—" His eyes soften and I see a flash of guilt in them

"Your paid maternity leave started an hour ago. Get. Your. Ass. Home."

"Sean, I told you that was unnecessary."

"Yeah, I chose to ignore you every single time you said it. It's the least I can do. You've got twelve months to spend with your son without having to worry about paying the mortgage or whether you can put food on the table."

"You're going to have to stop being nice or else I'm going to cry again," I say, tears already welling in my eyes. Damn pregnancy hormones.

Walking around the bar, he comes up beside me, putting his hands on my shoulders and turning me to face him. "You know Sam and I are always going to be here for you two. His father may be a poor excuse for a man," he says angrily, his head nodding to my stomach. "But the baby is always going to have us. Family comes in many different forms remember."

Fighting a losing battle with my emotions, I wrap my arms around Sean's back, burying my face in his shoulder and letting the tears fall. His arms close around my back and squeeze tight. "I mean it, Amz. You don't have to go through this alone and even if you want to, I would never let you."

When I'm all cried out, I let my arms drop down and move back, seeing Sean's 'do as I say' glare firmly in place.

"Yes, sir," I tease. It's not really a joke though considering Sean is a dom and Throb is actually a private sex club as well as a bar.

"I'm heading home to my wife and kids. Do you need a ride?"

"I'm just going to do the rounds and say goodbye to everyone then I promise I'll go home."

"All right. We're still on for dinner next week?"

"Definitely," I confirm.

"Good. Now do what you've got to do then get home and put your feet up. I know your blood pressure is down now but I want you to take care of yourself. For both of you." He reaches out and rubs my belly affectionately before kissing my cheek and walking back down the corridor toward his office.

I busy myself with wiping down the bar one last time before catching Jesse's eye from the other end of the bar and wave goodbye. Hooking my purse over my shoulder, I round the bar and come to a grinding halt when I see Thomas walking—okay it's more of a smoldering saunter—toward me.

"Hey, Amz," he says, a 'sexy and I know it' smile on his face and a tumbler of what I'm guessing is bourbon in his hand. His eyes aren't glassy though so he's definitely not drunk. I imagine he'd be totally shameless with some liquor in him. He's charming enough already, add a goofy drunken grin and uninhibited flirting and I'd be putty in his hands, *especially* since it's been nine months since I was last with a man. Seeing him all suave, sexy, and swoony—and in an open-necked business shirt and pants, no less—I decide to get in first, holding my hand up to stop him in his tracks.

"Before you say anything, no I'm not interested but I'm sure the club bunnies downstairs will eagerly take what you're offering," I reply with a smirk, crossing my arms around my 'way too big now' boobs.

His step falters and his eyes widen. "You're shooting me down before you even know what I was going to say?"

"I know your type, *playboy.*"

He stands there like a deer stuck in the headlights before shaking his head and quirking a brow.

"That's mighty presumptuous of you, sweetness. I was

coming to see how your last day at work was?" I started this smartass exchange, I'm going to have to finish it now to save face at the very least.

"Sweetness? Really?" I reply with mock disgust. Secretly, I kind of like that he has a nickname for me. Maybe not that one though, I've often thought Baby, Sweetheart, or Beautiful would sound amazing coming from his lips.

"It's better than calling you bitter and twisted." From anyone else that would be an asshole comment. From Thomas, with that salacious grin on his face, I know he's teasing.

I place my hand on his forearm and lightly run it down to his hand. I'm feeling rather feisty tonight, I wonder if I can blame it on the preggy hormones too.

"Oh honey, if you only knew how twisted I could be."

His eyes flash and he leans forward, bringing his body closer to mine. "Care to share? I'm a great listener."

"You couldn't handle me, Thomas Caldwell," I reply and damn if that doesn't make his eyes flash with heat. It's as if the world—and bar—around us have disappeared into a soundless vortex and we're the only two people in the room.

"I'd definitely be willing to give it a shot," he shoots back but the moment his abs touch my belly I'm instantly jolted out of his sexy force field.

"Um . . . did you forget something?" I ask, taking a step back and putting some much needed—by me—distance between us.

"What?" he asks, scrunching his forehead adorably.

No, not adorable. Not hot. Not anything. Chill your grill, Amy. Remember your current relationship status—totally and completely anti-men and anti-penis—for the indefinite future. Anti-everything that got me in my present physical condition.

My flight or fight instinct kicks in—albeit five minutes too late—and I know I need to extricate myself from this situation before I fall under his spell and beg him to kiss me, or touch me, and we all know that there's one big *massive* thing in the way of that, and his name is baby.

"I've gotta go," I quickly say. "Bye. Have a good night." I push past him and hurriedly make my way down the stairs—not an easy feat—and waddle down to the back of the club and out the staff entrance to safety.

Note to self—no more alone encounters with Thomas Caldwell until I'm ready to even contemplate a penis again, considering how well my *last* sexual encounter went.

I need to take sex out of the equation and remember what it's like to actually get to know a man without the obvious lead up to sex. I want those butterflies in my tummy, the tingles in those secret places that can't be seen, and that whoosh feeling only that something—and someone—special can bring.

I keep repeating 'butterflies, tingles, and whoosh' in my head as I sneak one last look over my shoulder at the man—without knowing it—that would have the power to make me forget myself and what I want in life with one 'come hither' smile.

Right now, all I want—all I'm going to have—is a life with me and my baby boy.

That's all I need for now. That's what I'm going to keep telling myself, anyway.

2

Thomas

Abstinence makes the heart grow stronger.

Nope. It makes the cock harder, the grip stronger, the nights longer, and you end up using your gym membership on a *very* regular basis.

Maybe it's because my heart hasn't found anyone worth skipping a beat for in my thirty-four years on this earth and I've purposefully avoided any situations where my past gregarious self could decide to come out and play.

My life is work, gym, home, sleep, wake up then repeat as per the day before.

As far as home is concerned, I now live by myself in the city. When Abi and Cade got married, and having already heard—and seen—far too much of those two in their newlywed bliss, I offered to move into Abi's apartment. It was a win/win for all of us. Abi didn't need to sell her former home and all the hard work it represents and I was able to escape their love—and sex—bubble.

Work has been a whole other challenge unto itself. It's

where my main focus has been. When the shit hit the fan with Cade's father a few months ago, Cade, his brother Cam, and sister Callie decided they'd had enough and walked away from their parents. They haven't had anything to do with them.

Since I worked for Cade Sr., I decided it was time to move on and take the big step of working for myself as a business consultant. Now, I'm hired to go into companies in trouble and restructure, refinance, and in some cases, close them down.

It's refreshing, it's definitely challenging, and more than anything else, rewarding.

So new work, new home, and a new appreciation for spending time in my own presence.

It's probably made my whole vow of abstinence at least a little bit easier. It's the last thing I ever thought I'd be doing, actually *choosing* to not have sex with any willing—and attractive—female that crosses my path, but getting chlamydia and then having to contact the last ten women I'd slept with to tell them that embarrassing fact was as fun as having a cotton swab stuck down my . . . yeah, I'd rather not remember that.

I'd almost go so far as to say abstinence has made my mind stronger, my focus sharper, and reinforced my determination to uphold my vow—and prove Cade wrong—that the next woman I sleep with will be the as yet elusive 'one.'

I thank *God* that my self-imposed sex ban does *not* discount masturbation. Had I been stupid enough to go *that* far, I'd have given up long ago.

Tonight is the guys' monthly poker night, and it's my turn to play host.

With snacks, drinks, and the Bulls' home game on the screen, I'm all set and ready to go when the intercom sounds and Cade's voice fills the room. "Thomas, you sad sack, let me in."

I walk over to the speaker by the front door and push the answer button. "I'm sorry, I've already got cable, hookers, and life insurance. I don't need whatever you're selling."

I hear laughter in response. "At least take your hand off it long enough to unlock the lobby door," our other friend Noah retorts.

"But I'm just getting to the good part," I reply as I push 1 on the keypad to open the door as requested.

"Make sure you wash your hands then," Noah's brother Matt shouts and a loud click comes down the line letting me know they've gained access to my building.

I make my way to the kitchen and wet my hands then return to open the front door, making a point to reach out and shake Matt's hand with a wicked grin on my face.

"Oh fuck, gross dude. I was just pulling your leg."

"And I was just pulling something else," I retort, stepping aside and sweeping my arm out to welcome them inside.

"Only you would make a vow of fucking abstinence with Cade and be determined to see it through. I don't know how you've lasted ten months."

"Self-control is a wondrous thing, young Matt," Sean says, wrapping his arm around Matt's shoulders and leading him to the table.

"Self-gratification is a hell of a lot better," I retort.

Sean is the owner of Throb, the club where Amy works—now in the office rather than behind the bar—and the rest of us frequent. He's married to Sam and together they have three children under seven. I bet he knows all about the important need for self-control, let alone the frustration of it.

"Are we playing poker or plaiting each other's hair and talking about all the selfish men in our lives?" Zach jibes.

That gets everyone laughing and after grabbing drinks, we make our way to the table.

"You guys might as well empty your pockets now because I'm feeling lucky tonight and Daddy needs a new set of golf clubs," Noah says with a shit-eating grin.

"Dream on, buddy," I reply, dealing out the first hand and settling in for what will no doubt be another entertaining—and hopefully lucrative—night with the guys.

"So what was up with Amy at the baby shower?" I ask, collecting my winnings from the last pot in the center of the table.

"What do you mean?" Cade asks.

"She didn't seem into it," I reply. I probably watched her a little too closely but it's true, Amy wasn't fully engaged in the festivities. She was there, she laughed at the right times, joined in on the conversation but something about her seemed closed off. Her smiles seemed guarded, her body taut as if ready to escape at any moment. Having thought about it afterward, she didn't seem completely comfortable with the occasion.

"She's a single woman who's about to become a single mom. Maybe it's starting to dawn on her what she's about to embark on," Cade says.

I take another swig of my beer. "It's a bit late for that though."

"She's a remarkable woman with more resilience than most women I know, our wives notwithstanding," Sean says. "She's got the girls though, and her dad and stepmother are very much a part of her life too."

"What's with the fascination with Amy, Thomas?" Daniel asks, leaning back in his chair and narrowing his eyes at me.

"Nothing," I reply with a shrug. "She's cool. I can't believe that she'd ever hook up with the type of guy to love and leave her. I hate assholes who don't face the consequences of their actions." *Considering I'm ten months into dealing with the aftermath of mine.*

"Believe me, there was no *love* in that encounter," Sean mutters under his breath.

"Who's the father then? You obviously know him," I continue. The room goes silent, and it's like I've just put a proverbial foot in my mouth.

I look around the table. Noah and Cade are having some magical silent conversation through wide eyes, Matt and Zach look amused, Daniel concentrates on shuffling the cards in his hands and Sean is leaning forward with his elbows resting on the table.

"Uh, why do I feel like I'm the last to know this?" I ask the group at large. "What's the big secret?"

"Out of respect for Amy," Sean says, "it's not really our place to tell you." For a normally straight up guy, his answer puzzles me.

"Do I *know* the guy? And you all know? Why do I feel like I'm missing out on the worst kept secret on earth?"

An awkward silence clouds the room and I'm about to open my mouth when Cade steps in.

"Thomas, you've gotta understand. Sean is in a difficult position here. He's her boss. There's things he probably hasn't told any of us about when it comes to Amy."

"Are you *just* her boss?" I ask, getting a horrible feeling but knowing it couldn't *possibly* be true.

"What does *that* mean?" Sean asks, his voice menacing.

I quickly put my hands up in surrender. "Whoa, dude. I just meant you seem rather involved."

"Involved?" he growls.

"In her business . . ." I explain.

"She's worked for me for over five years now. She's the only employee that has been there that long. She's been dealt an unexpected *hand* . . ." His lips twitch as Daniel deals us all new cards.

"What does that even mean?" I press.

"Amy has always kept things close to her chest. She's not as loud and brash as the rest of the girls and in some ways is quite introverted, in others she's rather in your face. If you annoy her or do any of her friends wrong, she'll be on you like white on rice and *not* in a good way," Matt explains, a wry smile playing on his lips. "It's probably Mia's influence."

"She's always been staunchly protective of those close to her," Sean says.

"Hopefully she realizes she's got a lot of people in her corner," Noah adds and we all nod in agreement.

Something inside of me hates that such a nice, decent, loyal woman is going through this alone. We're not close and we haven't had another deep and meaningful conversation since that night months ago when she gave me a little light on what was not an easy night.

But nobody should be alone—or feel like they are—when they're embarking on what should be one of the best experiences of their life, one that they'll remember forever.

I do know one thing, when I find out who the asshole is

who walked away from his child, I'll be ready and waiting to make him understand just how epic his fuck up is. Because I'm one of the lucky kids that was walked away from as a toddler but was thankfully adopted by amazing parents when I was eight years old.

I'm determined. The next time I see Amy, I'm going to make more of an effort to be her friend.

In whatever capacity she needs.

3

Amy

The following Thursday I'm standing alone, a million months pregnant, and my waters decide that this would be the most perfect moment in the world to imitate Niagara Falls in the cereal aisle of the grocery store. Nine p.m. and all I want is some Lucky Charms and Reese's Peanut Butter Cups.

Is it not too much to ask to be allowed to soothe a craving I've had all freaking day without the child that I love and adore making their impending arrival known in the most embarrassing way possible?

"Amy?" *Ah fuck on a shit stick.*

I know that voice. I've fantasized nightly over that voice, though I'd never tell *him* that.

Turning my head, I see the object of my secret desire but the continuing geyser of amniotic fluid dripping between my thighs snaps me out of my daze, mortification coursing through me.

Of all the fucking people to see me at my lowest most embarrassing point, it would have to be *him.* It's like those nightmares you have about walking through high school with your skirt tucked into your underwear or getting your period when you're least expecting it.

Why did I have to wear a skirt?

Clean-up on aisle five. *Literally.*

"Thomas . . ."

He tilts his head, his eyes narrowing at me.

"Are you all right?" Shit. Now he's being kind of nice. What the hell do I do with that?

"I'm peach—" I say just as my stomach clenches in displeasure, or simply preparation.

In the blink of an eye he's at my side, his arm around my waist as my knees buckle and with nothing else to do, I sag into him. "Amy, what's wrong?"

Before I can say anything to him, my entire stomach clenches, lightning bolts of pain shooting across and down through my lady bits. I'm not with it enough to realize I haven't hit the floor, two strong arms catching me and gently easing me down until I'm sitting on something—or someone.

"Ahhh shit fuck mother freaking damn," I grind out, my hand instinctively wrapping around my ginormous belly.

He snorts and my head snaps to glare at him. "Right. Message received. Don't laugh at the pregnant woman."

"A pregnant woman who's currently going into labor," I explain.

"Shit," he whispers, his face turning ashen. "We need to get you to the hospital, doctor, some sort of medical professional. Cade, or Noah, Mac even. She's a nurse and she's had a baby already. She'll do."

"Excuse me?" a male voice asks from above us. I look up to see a good-looking middle-aged man in store uniform standing next to us, cell phone in hand. "Do you need me to call 911?"

"That would be great," Thomas says, moving his legs apart so I ease between them onto the floor.

"Stay there, we'll get help for you," he says before rushing down the aisle and out of sight.

Thankfully having a small window in between contractions, I put my hand on his arm and squeeze to get his attention. "Thomas. I need you to stay calm."

"Calm? *Calm?* You're about to give birth on a dirty grocery store floor. How the hell are *you* calm?"

"You were fine before," I reply, in no way resembling anything but calm on the inside. I don't want my baby born in a grocery store.

"That was before your body contorted like a demon possessed and you told me you were in labor which means you need. Medical. Care," he bites out. Yet again I feel the tell-tale clenching of my uterus and I dig my nails into his forearms. This time it's stronger, the pain reaching a fast crescendo, causing a whimper to escape my lips.

"Fuck this. I'm taking you to the hospital myself."

"It's not supposed to happen like this. It's too fast. I'm not due for four weeks."

"I know enough to know that your water breaking means it *is* happening and soon. Let's get you to my car and I'll take you myself. I'll ring Cade on the way. He can help me help you."

I practice my Lamaze breathing, wishing I'd actually finished all of the classes or demanded that Abi escort me everywhere after thirty-five weeks in the event that this actually happened.

The pain ebbs away and I take some desperately needed deep breaths, knowing that it's only going to be a short reprieve until another contraction hits.

"Thomas?"

"Is another one coming?" In a moment when I never thought it would ever be possible to laugh, a husky snort escapes my lips.

"Not yet, but I'm betting it might not be long."

"You ready to move?"

"Nope."

He reaches his hand around and gently cups my jaw, pushing my face around so I meet his eyes. "As much as I like having a gorgeous woman in my lap, maybe not so much when she's about to give birth and should really be . . . I dunno . . . heading to the hospital?"

It's then that another contraction jolts through me, no slow growing warning this time.

"Fuck fuck fuck fuck fuck. . . . ing firetruck."

Thomas links his fingers with mine this time, his arms cocooning me. I don't feel like I'm going through this alone and lo and fucking behold, I'm glad he's here with me.

"Breathe, sweetness." And I do. I breathe, I pant, I scream, I cry, and then repeat all of the above until the pain passes again.

I drop my head back, burying my forehead in Thomas's neck, struggling to get my breathing under control.

"We have a bit of an audience," he murmurs against my hair and I sigh in frustration but right at that moment, it's the last thing on my mind. "You also swear like a sailor when you're in labor."

"I wouldn't know," I reply breathlessly. "Never had my body make me birth a baby before."

That earns me a chuckle but I'm already too tired to give a shit.

Footsteps come toward us, getting louder against the vinyl floor, I don't bother looking up though.

"The EMTs should be here shortly. They said just to keep her comfortable and help her through the contractions," I hear from beside me, recognizing the grocery store clerk's voice.

"Thanks. Can you bring us a bottle of water and a towel or something? I'd like to get her off this floor if possible."

"I can try and bring an office chair or something? Would that help?"

"Worth a shot," Thomas replies.

"Not moving," I mumble, not bothering to open my eyes let alone lift my head from his neck.

"Sweetness, we've got to get you off this floor."

"Not. Moving," I grind out, my hands clenching his as another contraction wracks my body again.

"Not. Supposed. To. Happen. Like. This," I spit out between pants.

"I know," Thomas replies tightly, his body firm behind mine, cradling me as I breathe.

I rant and rock in place, trying everything I can just to get through what I know is the most natural thing in the world. I just *really* wish it wasn't happening in the cereal aisle of the grocery store.

I feel another gush of fluid seeping out from between my legs.

Can this get any more mortifying?

"I feel like I need to move but I *really* don't want to," I whisper hoarsely into Thomas's ear, my head making its way back to its new home in the crook of his neck.

He releases one of my hands and lifts his fingers up to brush away the damp hair now clinging to my face. "You're doing so well, Amz. I can't imagine what it's like for you, but you're handling everything like a champ."

"A champ at what? Creating a birth story my son will never forget?" I reply with a laugh.

"Well, there is *that.*"

"Can you grab my phone? I need to call Mia. She's supposed to be my birthing partner but the way this is going, you might've just walked yourself into the role."

"Right now, I wouldn't want to be anywhere else," he says quietly, just for me to hear and for the first time in a long time, I don't doubt the sincerity of his words. It's not a line and it's exactly what I need in that moment and I forget all about calling anyone.

"Thomas . . ." I say but that now familiar tightening between my legs, my stomach, and my back makes a return but this time it feels different.

There's an urgency to it, a previously unfelt need to move, to do something, to push.

"Shit shit shit shit," I say between pants, Thomas's arms tightening around my chest, our hands entwined again, and my head drops down to my chest.

"Where the hell are those paramedics?" Thomas grinds out.

The store manager returns with a pile of towels, his face tight, his eyes widen and jerking around, looking anywhere except to me.

Thomas reaches out a hand to grab the linen. Somehow, my impromptu birthing partner manages to lift my hips up and places the towels under me, spreading them out to cover most of the floor beneath me.

"How you doing, sweetness?" he asks softly, running his hand down my cheek, my jaw, turning my face toward him, his forehead coming down to rest on mine.

"You're a superstar," he whispers.

"I'm glad you're here," I reply and his eyes crinkle.

"The ambulance will be here soon, we'll go to the hospital and soon you'll meet your son."

"I can't wait." Tears well in my eyes, yet still I can't look away from Thomas.

"You've just gotta hold on, Amz. We're gonna get you sorted and then you'll be holding your baby boy in your arms."

And again, a contraction hits, but this time it's stronger, more crippling, but yet, an overwhelming feeling washes over me.

I need to push.

1 . . . 2 . . . 3 . . . shit shit shit. This is happening. On a grocery store floor.

I'm going to give birth on a freaking grocery store floor.

In what universe would this ever be okay? Releasing Thomas.

"Thomas, I need to push."

"What?" he gasps. I turn my head to meet his eyes.

"You've got to hold on. Help is coming."

"I need to push," I grind out, squeezing his fingers so tight I swear I could break them.

Instinctively I reach down between my legs, my hand delving inside my underwear. I gasp when I not only feel the wetness left from my water breaking but immense pressure and pushing slightly inside, a hard round . . . head.

"Thomas . . ." I say, my voice strained, worried, scared. "Help me take these off." I grab my underwear and tear them down my legs.

Thomas's fingers take over and he leans around my torso to pull my panties the rest of the way off. He grabs a towel from the pile beside us—man the manager went overboard—and drapes it over my legs as I hike my skirt up.

"Why is this happening to me? It shouldn't be this fast, I should have hours to go," I tell him.

"What do you need me to do?" he asks, sitting beside me as I brace my arms behind me, holding my body up.

By now, preserving my dignity is the last thing on my mind. It's looking like I'm about to give birth in front of a bunch of strangers, who, I might add, don't seem to be rushing to my aid.

"Thomas, I need you to help me. I've got to . . . puuuuu-ussssshhhhh," I breathe out. I lean forward and grab hold of my knees, keeping myself upright while panting through yet another contraction. They're coming hard and fast now and I know—just *know*—that my son is in a hurry to enter the world.

"Ah . . . what do I do?" he asks, scooting around me on his knees and looking down at me.

"I need you to help me guide him out. Shit, this hurts like a motherfucking bitch."

He moves down my body until he positions himself smack bang between my legs, his eyes going wide as he gets the money shot—not the good kind of course—but an unfettered view of my vagina.

I know what happens to lady parts during pregnancy. I even got a mirror to have a look down there a few weeks ago because part of my inquisitive brain needed to see all of the body changes happening to me.

His eyes are wide, his face flushed as he sits down and braces his legs outside of mine, grounding me.

"You tell me when you're ready to push and we'll do this."

"I don't have a clue what I'm doing," I pant and his lips twitch.

"That makes two of us, sweetness, but women have been doing this for years. Your body will know what to do, we'll just follow its lead."

And right now, I wish I could kiss the man because every word out of his mouth is the honest to God truth and it's just the motivation I need to get through this—not that I really have a choice in the matter.

"Oh my—shit . . . here comes another one."

"Another what?" he asks an octave higher than normal, eyes darting down between my legs then quickly back up again.

"Contraction!" My voice is now shrill as pain sears through me.

"Breathe, Amz. Just keep on breathing."

"I feel like the chick from Aliens. I swear. . . . this . . . baby . . . is trying . . . to claw . . . his way . . . out. Holy fuckballs!"

Thomas's hands hook my legs up so my feet are resting on his chest, eyes locked with mine. He looks as terrified as I feel on the inside, underneath the swearing and freaking out of course.

But I think it's all valid considering right now all I can feel is this huge pressure pushing down deep in my pelvis, and another overwhelming need to push comes over me.

"I've gotta pushhhh," I grind out between gritted teeth as I press my hands hard against the floor, brace my feet on Thomas's shoulders and do what my body is screaming at me to do, and that's push.

"Breathe, sweetness," he says and I do, gulping down air like a mad woman as I keep pushing, panting, and pushing again.

His hands move between my legs, his eyes glued to the party place where all the action is happening. "I can see his head, Amz. You're doing so fucking well." He glances up at me, his eyes filled with awe and—oh my God, is he crying?

The contraction subsides and my chest heaves as I try to calm my breathing. It feels like a giant watermelon has set up shop in my cervix, the pressure so immense it's almost unbearable.

Not even a minute passes before I'm ready to go ahead.

"Where the hell are those paramedics?" I groan and Thomas rubs my legs again, kneading my calf muscles gently.

"I don't think we're gonna need them. He's just sitting there waiting for one last go, Amy. You can do this. You're a total birthing rock star," he says and the soft expression on his face and—yes, his wet eyes—totally reassure and egg me on.

I start my Lamaze breathing, footsteps come at me from the side and a quick turn of my head brings me face to face with a smiling lady paramedic.

"Looks like we got here in time for the good bit. You ready to meet your baby?" she says to me before smiling at Thomas. I realize what she must think but right now, correcting her is the *least* of my worries.

I nod then focus on the task at hand, meeting Thomas's approving eyes and huge smile—albeit a slightly tight, worried one—as the paramedic scoots in behind me, giving me a much-needed body to anchor myself to.

Then it's on like Donkey Kong. Pain slices through me, my hands shooting out and gripping the paramedic's legs, sweat beading off my face as I push. . . . and push . . . my chin digging into my chest and tears pouring from my eyes as I continue to push, unable to breathe because my sole focus right now is to meet my much-loved baby boy.

"Fuck fuck fuck fuck fuck, damn, shit, holy mother of all this . . . fuuuuuuccccckkkk. . . ." I give one last push until there's nothing left of me, collapsing back against the woman who's thankfully strong and sturdy at my back as a piercing cry fills the air with a round of applause following shortly after.

Calling up the last ounce of strength I have in me, I lift my head and see the most beautiful sight of my life, Thomas Caldwell cradling my newborn son, all slimy and covered in afterbirth, with wet eyes and the most dazzling smile I've ever seen.

"What's his name?" he asks, wrapping my baby in the clean towel handed to him by a male paramedic who magically appears from nowhere.

Thomas's voice is soft and gentle. It's *so* unlike anything I've ever heard from him. It's almost reverent and if I wasn't so fucking exhausted from pushing a baby out of my vagina, I could totally fall in love with that kind of voice.

"Brody," I whisper, watching through glassy eyes as Thomas lowers his head and plants a kiss on my son's forehead.

"Well hey there, Brody. Let me introduce you to your mama."

4

Thomas

Holy crap, I've just put my hand into a woman's vagina and it had nothing to do with sex and everything to do with bringing a slimy, crying, amazing baby boy into the world.

And it was the most beautiful moment of my thirty-four-year life.

I helped bring new life into the world. No training and no fucking clue what the hell I was doing. I just held my hands there and guided him out while Amy did all the hard work.

Amy, she was fucking amazing. Awe-inspiring, strong, focused, steady as a fucking stone.

I'm totally and utterly lost for words. My eyes are wet with tears and I don't give a fuck who sees.

I bundle the baby up in the last clean towel we have and when the other paramedic carefully lowers Amy's legs from my chest, I walk forward on my knees and carefully place her son in her arms.

Heart—blown. Mind—blown. Any preconceptions I had about my life and my future—totally fucking blown.

One minute, you're going about your life without a care in the world, shopping for Lucky Charms, the next you're coming to the aid of a woman and sharing this profound, life-changing moment together.

I call Cade and Abi and then Mia from the ambulance as we make our way to the hospital, asking Cade to swing by the grocery store to grab my car as well as a change of clothes since I'm wearing a scrub top the paramedics sorted me out with.

An hour later, Amy and the baby are settled in a bed in the maternity ward and I'm sitting in the family room waiting for everyone to arrive.

Abi and Mia arrive first, Mia enveloping me in a hug when they reach my side.

"So glad you were there, Thomas. I can't imagine what it would've been like for her if she was alone."

"There was the friendly store manager who couldn't disappear fast enough after he realized what was going on," I reply with a chuckle, looking down the hall to see Cade coming our way.

"You look exhausted," he says to me when he reaches us, holding my spare car key out for me.

"You get that when you go to the grocery store for a late night snack and end up delivering a baby."

"It's definitely going to be a story you tell your grandkids, that's for sure," he replies with a smile. "By the way, I parked your car in my staff parking space. Just use my name when you leave."

"Thanks for that. My quiet night kind of got hijacked and my car was the least of my worries."

"Did you at least get your snack?" Abi asks, wrapping her arm around my waist and hugging my side.

Looking down at her, I narrow my eyes. "In between catching Amy to stop her falling on the floor and getting to know her intimately in a *very* unexpected way? It kind of escaped my mind."

"Lucky I bought you something to eat then, isn't it," she replies with a grin, stepping away and handing over a bag that smells divine.

"I love you. Leave your husband and run away with me," I say, giving Abi my best puppy dog eyes.

"Oh shut it. You know I love you but I love my doctor more." She looks over at Cade and winks at him, earning a chuckle from all of us.

A tall, surprisingly built and somewhat familiar mid-fifties man walks down the hall toward us, a huge grin on his face and a petite curvy blond woman who couldn't be a day past forty on his arm.

"Gareth!" Abi cries, letting me go and tackling the couple before they can take the time to brace. Then I remember seeing them at the baby shower last week; Amy's dad and stepmother.

"Whoa, Abi-Jane. Give a man a chance to prepare," Gareth wheezes with a grin.

Abi moves her attention to Amy's stepmother, Kristy, wrapping her arms around her shoulders and squeezing tight.

"Grandpa and Grandma," she says, her voice uncharacteristically hoarse.

"Yeah, you can stop that talk right now. I'm going to be the cool grandma, one with a cool name like Gam Gam or Nana Kris," Kristy replies.

Gareth steps forward and shakes Cade's hand, moving on to give Mia a quick hug before turning his attention to me.

"You Thomas?" he asks, all eyes turning to the two of us.

"Yes, sir. Thomas Caldwell." I offer my hand out but he doesn't shake it like I expect, instead he grabs my hand and jerks me forward, wrapping an arm around my shoulders for a firm back slap.

"Call me Gareth. Thank you for being there for my girl and grandson." My throat tightens and I quickly swallow down the startings of a lump as he lets me go and looks me straight in the eye.

Respect. Pride. Gratitude.

"I was glad she had someone there to help."

He grasps my hand and holds tight, his gaze boring into mine. "You made sure they were safe, that *she* was looked after, and you brought my grandson into the world. Apart from her stepmother, she's my world, and now my grandson is too. I owe you everything, Thomas."

"You're welcome," I reply, my voice gruff.

"Right," Gareth announces, "time for me to meet the next Bears' linebacker!"

"You look like you need a drink," Cade says once everyone else has gone to see Amy.

I finally succumb to the exhaustion I've been holding back, everything I'm feeling—the exhilaration, the adrenaline high, the complete and utter mind fuck of the night's activities—wash over me. "You got a secret stash of bourbon somewhere, Carsen?" I ask.

He chuckles and winks. "You'd be surprised at what you can find around here. Let's go."

Bumping my shoulder as he passes, he walks down the hall and I follow. A short detour to the ground floor and the doctor's locker room, and a return ride up to the rooftop later, the two of us are sitting on the roof of the hospital looking out over the lights of the city we call home.

I take a swig from the hip flask Cade swiped and hand it back to him, wincing a little at the smooth welcome burn as I swallow. "That was kind of epic. Seeing her go through that, being there to help her, bringing a new life into the world."

"I still remember every single birth I've been at. It puts everything into perspective."

"You're telling me."

"Well I just did, but carry on," he muses.

"She's so strong. I can't imagine what it would've been like to go through that alone."

"Lucky you suck at adulting and needed to buy food late at night."

"She shouldn't have had to be there tonight. She was pregnant and *grocery shopping* at ten o'clock at night. She should've had someone looking out for her, protecting her, just *being* there . . ."

"She's a good woman."

"Then why the fuck is she doing this all alone?"

His head turns toward me, meeting my eyes. "She's not. She's got us, her father, her stepmom . . ."

"You know what I mean, Cade." He sighs and looks back out to the view.

"Because given the choice of being a man and walking away, the baby's father made the right choice for everybody."

My head jerks back at his answer, which wasn't really an answer at all. "How the fuck is walking away from your child, your own flesh and blood, the right choice? If you have sex and don't use protection, everyone involved knows the consequences. He made that choice, she made that choice, why should Amy be the only one taking responsibility?"

"Believe me when I say that it was and—in his case—always will be, the best thing he ever did," Cade says quizzically.

"Who is it, Carsen?"

"It's not my place," he says quickly.

"Maybe not, but somebody needs to hunt him down, kick his ass then sterilize him, just for good measure."

"Remind me never to get on your bad side."

I snort at that because in all of the fifteen years that I've known the guy, not once has Cade ever let me down, and vice versa.

Comfortable silence stretches between us and I welcome it, my mind still reeling from the events of the night.

"Is that why you've kept going with the abstinence thing?" he says. "Because you're taking responsibility for your actions?"

I ponder his words, and he's right, and he's wrong. But I'm not sure exactly how to explain it.

"Yes and no. The STD was definitely a huge wake-up call for me, but now, it's just hitting me that I could've been that guy, one who's faced with the decision to stay or walk away."

"You wouldn't ever walk away from a child," Cade says without hesitation.

"No, I couldn't but . . ." I take a moment to gather my thoughts. "I want what you've got, what Dan and Noah have.

A family, a partner, a wife, a fucking plan at least. By taking sex out of the equation, I've been able to focus on my business, building my brand and my reputation, and not once have I regretted my vow, but tonight something clicked. It's not all about the physical stuff. There's something deeper I want, maybe even need."

Cade's surprisingly quiet for a while, actually for-fucking-ever by his standards, before he stands up and holds his hand out to help me up. "Either Amy kicked you in the head during the birth, or you've had a profound, life-changing moment while guiding a seven-pound baby out of her—"

"Yeah, yeah. Feel free to stop giving me crap at *any* time now."

"I'm not fucking with you. You deserve to have what we have. I *want* you to find that."

I meet his eyes and all I see is truth and now it's my turn to be quiet as the warring emotions in my head fight for supremacy.

The most overwhelming one, the one I can't ignore even if I wanted to, is the instinctive desire to be there for Amy. To help her in any way I can. To be that man at her back, the one looking out for her—and now Brody—protecting her, just being *there* for her.

Tonight we had a moment and she may not realize the significance of that yet, but I'm damn well going to make sure that she does.

My father always told me that good things take time, effort, and a hell of a lot of trouble.

Somehow in this case it's going to take all of that and then some to get to the good stuff.

And for some insane reason—maybe it's the whiskey, the

lack of sleep, or the adrenaline high—but I'm suddenly really looking forward to giving it a try.

It was after everyone else had gone that I knocked gently on the door to Amy's hospital room, easing it open slowly to see her sitting up in the bed, Brody bundled up in a blue blanket, safely cradled in her arms.

"Come in," she whispers, just loud enough for me to hear.

I step inside and close the door behind me before making my way over to her side.

"Hey," I say, my eyes locked with her soft ones, a lazy smile gracing her lips as I stop beside her, reaching out to run my index finger down the side of Brody's head.

"Thank you for staying with me, for helping me."

"It was amazing and scary, and I was freaking out, but it all worked out in the end, didn't it, little man?"

"He looks good on you."

My eyes meet hers and I have to admit, I like the way she's watching me, the way her words make me feel.

"He's definitely an attention getter. Look at the way he came into the world," I say with a grin.

"It's surreal. A few hours ago I was craving peanut butter cups and Lucky Charms, and instead of getting either, I gave birth in the cereal aisle."

"Just think, you could've called him Lucky."

"Oh God," she says with a laugh. "That would be horrific."

"What about Cheerio?"

"No, stop!" She's giggling now, her face radiant. Fuck, Caldwell. Calm down already.

"What's wrong?" she asks, tilting her head to the side and studying me. "Your expression changed all of a sudden."

"This night has just been a bit of a mind fuck." I wince, looking down at the baby in my arms. "Sorry, little man."

Amy snorts and shakes her head, a smile playing on her lips. "I think you're fine considering he's not even a day old and he can't cogitate or even understand anything we say."

"Duly noted," I reply, her happiness contagious.

"I get what you mean though," she says quietly.

Out of unspoken need—maybe even instinct—I sit down on the side of the bed, reaching out and rubbing my fingers over hers before entwining them. I don't know why I do it, or what it even means, but it centers me in what has been a crazy wild night, one that I'm sure to remember for a long time.

"You doing okay?" I ask, squeezing her hand gently.

Her gaze lifts from our joined hands to my face, big glassy blue eyes meeting mine as she bites her lip. "I'm a mom."

My mouth tips up. "You definitely are, sweetness."

"When did *that* happen?"

Lifting my other hand up, I check my watch. "About four hours ago."

"He's here . . ." she says, her voice full of wonder.

"And both of you are amazing," I say, my attention flicking between Amy and her peacefully sleeping son.

"Am I gonna be able to do this?" Her eyes meet mine and I see the warring emotions hidden behind them.

And just like that, she's got me hooked. With those eight words, there's no way in hell I'd ever want to—let alone be able to—walk away now. Because I know what it's like to have no father and I know what it's like to have the best dad in the world.

If Amy lets me, I'm giving myself the job of being there for Brody and his mother. I'm going to do what the poor-excuse-for-a-man sperm donor was too gutless to do. I'll be their rock, I'll be their anchor, and I'm going to be the man who'll *always* put her first . . . *them* first.

I flex my fingers in hers and squeeze her hand, leaning down to first kiss Brody's forehead then lifting my head to do the same to his mother. "You already are, and whenever you think you're not, I'm going to be right there beside you making sure you know you can."

A lone tear falls down Amy's cheek and with my thumb, I brush it away, not once breaking eye contact. "I'm glad you're here," she whispers.

"There isn't anywhere else I'd rather be."

5

SIX WEEKS POST GROCERY STORE BIRTH

Amy

"We still on for tomorrow night?"

"What's tomorrow night?" Mia asks from beside me where she's lounging on my sofa, remote in hand as she scrolls through the channels on the TV.

"New season of *The Bachelor* starts next week. We need to start a new fantasy draft."

"You really need to get out more Amz," she says with a giggle.

"Yeah," I reply, tilting my head toward Brody who's lying on his back underneath his play gym. "I'll get right on that."

"Who else is coming?"

"Just Abi, Zoe, Nat, and Kristy."

"Ooh, so we'll all get a good spread of picks then."

"We will indeed."

"Are you staying for dinner tonight or does your husband and daughter want to see you?" I ask.

"I'm staying and we're ordering in. It's best friend etiquette."

My brows shoot up. "You sure? You don't have to stay, hun. You've got your family to get back to."

She leans over and puts her hand on my arm. "Amz, having a child doesn't mean you have to stop living your life. Matt is more than capable of watching Emma. In fact, they're having a daddy-daughter date at Lincoln Park Zoo. Mommy is having a best friend date with Aunty Amy, gorging on takeout, and doing her research so she gets only the best eligible women for our bachelor's lonely heart." By the end of her speech, she has her hand over her heart and is looking at me with a fake dreamy expression.

I giggle, shaking my head as I get down on my knees and crawl over to Brody and kiss his forehead. I sit back on my butt and lift him up, cradling him in my arms, needing my next baby hit. Turning his head, he nuzzles my shirt, looking for food and setting off my let down like practiced clockwork.

I scooch back to my chair and pull myself up, getting comfortable while simultaneously pulling up my top and unclasping the cup of my nursing bra with one hand.

"Look at you go. You're a pro at nursing now," Mia says as I move Brody's head toward the motherland of milk known as my nipple. I grin and watch Brody latch on.

"So . . . Thomas . . ." Mia says quietly, dragging out his name.

"Yes . . ." My eyes drift over to her, wondering where she's going with this.

"What's up with *that?*" she asks, tilting her head toward the kitchen where the man in question is cleaning up.

"He's just helping out." My eyes drift to the doorway before moving back to my best friend.

"Helping out? Amz, it's been six weeks. There's helping

out and then there's *that.*" She tilts her head at the kitchen leaving me in no doubt what *that* is. She doesn't stop there though. "He cleans, he cooks, and he *sits* here at your beck and call. That's more than 'helping out.'"

I shrug and feeling Brody pull off, run my hand up to cradle his head and guide him back to my nipple.

"At first I figured it was just him helping out like the rest of us. But you guys were never that close, well I didn't think you were. And now—*now*—he's still around and he's *still* doing dishes and stuff. It's so far from the Thomas I know, it's not funny . . . well, it is, but—"

I stifle a giggle but have to stop her before she says something bad. "Meems . . ."

She snaps her mouth shut and stares at me, her eyes going from narrowed contemplation to wide surprise. "Oh my God, no. . . ."

It was a statement, not a question and one I'm not quite sure how to answer. To me, he's just Thomas Caldwell. Good cook, good guy, and freaking awesome at catching a baby in a grocery aisle.

"When I had Brody and Thomas was there, something kinda happened between us."

"While you were giving *birth?*" she asks, her hushed voice rises to a squeak.

"No!" I stage whisper back, looking down to check that my baby boy is still sleeping, he's not, instead his bright blue eyes—my eyes—are staring adoringly up at me while he continues to nurse.

"Then what is it? And why are you only telling me about this now? I've seen you at least three times a week since then and not *once* have you said that there was anything going on between you two."

"There's *nothing* going on between us. I've just given birth for God's sake. It's just . . . oh, I don't know."

She narrows her eyes at me, and I know I'm not going to get out of this without explaining.

"We're just connected now. There's something to be said about sharing a surreal and deep experience together that just . . . it just makes you see someone in a new light," I say with a shrug.

"Amz, I—"

"No, Meems. It's not anything like that. I'm a single mom with a newborn baby. He was there when Brody came into the world and since then, he's been here for me." She opens her mouth to say something but snaps it shut. "And it's not romantic, not for him. It's just—"

"How do you know it's not for him?" she says.

"Because it's never been like that between us. We were friendly acquaintances, then I could say that we became loose friends because of all of you. Now . . ."

"Is it romantic for *you?*"

"I don't know what it is. Not once has he let me down since Brody's birth. He said he'd be there for the two of us and he has been. Every single time he said he'd be here, he's been true to his word. Even late at night when it would normally just be me and Brody, he's stayed to keep me company, offering adult conversation that isn't all about the baby."

Mia looks meaningfully back toward the kitchen, her lips morphing from pursed into a slow smile when she turns back to me.

"You *sure* there's nothing romantic there?"

"He's just Thomas. He's always just been Thomas." Then, because it's Mia and she's one of the biggest meddlers I know, I lie. "I don't know if I'd want things to change."

Liar, liar, pants on fire.

The night after I got home from the hospital, Thomas was knocking on my door.

Since then, he's called or come over every few days. And don't get me started on how utterly adorable he's been with Brody.

The first moment I *wished* things were different with Thomas, Brody was two weeks old and had been up most of the day, refusing to sleep unless he was on me. It was the growth spurt from hell and I was grumpy, tired, hangry, and desperate for a shower lasting longer than a minute. When I heard the doorbell ring, I was literally ready to throttle the person behind the door.

Thomas took one look at me and didn't waste any time in taking Brody out of my arms and ushering me toward the bathroom. When I emerged twenty glorious minutes later, Brody was lying in his crib almost asleep and there was a ham salad sandwich waiting for me on the coffee table.

And for a brief moment, I caught a glimpse of a life where I wasn't a single mom and I had a partner who'd have my back when times were tough.

I'm jerked back to reality when Brody pulls off my nipple again. Knowing he's had enough, I quickly tuck my breast back into my bra, clasping the cup and pulling down my top before lifting him up and propping him up against my chest, rubbing gentle circles on his back.

"I like this," she says, her whole face now bright, almost hopeful. *Oh no.*

I narrow my eyes at her. "Mia Taylor, don't go getting any ideas. He's just being a good friend."

"Thomas is a great guy, he's awesome. He has his own business, he's settled and not going anywhere anytime soon, he has his own apartment, he's *single* and—"

"Abstinent," I say deadpan.

She throws her hand up nonchalantly. "Meh. The difference between abstinence and jumping back on the horse is one flash of those sexy milk jugs of yours."

"Mia!" I hiss.

"What? You two would be good together. He's definitely a step up from the sperm donor, that's for fucking sure."

"Remember what happened the last time I let my vagina make decisions for me?"

"Vaginas make mistakes, but they can also be fucking geniuses. Look what happened when I finally listened to mine."

"Yours just made you pull your head out of your ass and see what the rest of us already knew."

"Oh, I saw wood all right, a *lot* of it. Still do in fact," she replies with a laugh.

"Too much information. You've already informed me the 'mini' in mini WD is a gross understatement. That's all I need to know about your baby daddy."

Her face goes soft, her expression turning dreamy.

"Oh stop with the mushy happy face."

She turns to me with the same look. "Amz, you'll have reason to look like this one day. You of all people deserve a man that'll make you happy and give you lots and lots of orgasms. Until then, let your fingers do the walking and your trusty vibrator do the talking. I promise you, your vagina will thank you for it."

"Brody is only six weeks. There has been no walking or talking or anything even close to that with my vagina."

"Did I hear someone say vagina?" that deep caramel topped voice I may or may not hear in my dreams says. Both Mia and I snap our mouths shut, our eyes moving to the side of the room where the sexy—in no way is he getting anywhere near my vagina—man of the hour leans against the doorframe. He's holding a dishtowel in his hand and I can honestly say that there isn't anything I've seen lately more titillating than that image.

I really need to get out more if *that* is doing it for me. It's a freaking dishtowel for Christ's sake.

"I bet *you* like vaginas," Mia says, looking up at him with a smirk.

"I think any straight male does."

"Even abstinent ones?" she presses. My eyes snap to hers and if looks could kill, she'd be gravely wounded at the very least.

Thomas throws his head back and laughs. "Believe me, whether I'm having sex or not, I'll always be a fan."

"Happy vagina, happy life, I say," Mia adds.

I turn apologetic eyes to Thomas. "I'm sorry, Mia doesn't have a filter."

"I do too! I hate the word but I'm with Thomas, I'm a huge fan of the body part. Thankfully my husband is too."

"I think that's my cue to leave," Thomas says, turning to put the dishtowel on the kitchen counter and back to face me. "Is there anything I can get you before I go?"

I can't deny that my belly does a mini whoosh at the offer.

The last few months have seen Thomas stay true to his word about helping me with Brody. I honestly didn't expect him to follow through.

Not because he didn't want to, but because he didn't need to. I didn't ask, in fact, it's felt a little weird—but in a good way—spending so much time with him.

Before Brody's birth, our interactions have been brief at best. Don't get me wrong, I would've had to have been dead not to see how hot he is. I'm not—or I wasn't—in the right head space or right place in my life in general to consider anything with him. Let alone contemplate the possibility that he'd want anything with me. Pregnant with another man's child? It's not high on the list of desired women.

"Ah . . . Amz? You still with us?" Mia muses. I turn wide eyes her way before realizing I never answered Thomas.

I look over at him. "I'm good. And thank you for doing the kitchen, you really didn't have to."

His gaze pins me in place. "Said I would, sweetness. It's just cleaning. You have your hands full with Brody." He closes the distance between us, stopping just short of touching me.

"But—" I say, tilting my head up to watch him.

"What did I say?" he says softly like he only wants me to hear.

"I know," I acquiesce, my breath catching as he bends and rests a hand on the back of my chair. His head dips and he kisses the top of Brody's head—bigger whoosh—then mine. *Mega whoosh.*

"Anything you need, anytime you need it, Amz. I said it and I meant it. Now do me a favor and just sit back and *relax,*" he murmurs against my skin, his warm breath fanning over me. It takes everything I have not to shiver.

He straightens and meets my eyes, giving me a meaningful nod before moving over to Mia and kissing her cheek.

"You two enjoy your *Bachelor* draft planning and feel free to continue discussing my favorite female body part in my absence." My cheeks heat—something he doesn't miss if the knowing glint in his eye is anything to go by—but he doesn't call me on it. He simply grins and leaves the room.

"Maybe I *do* have to pop home," Mia blurts out as soon as he's gone.

"You do?" I ask, turning back toward her as I adjust a now sleeping baby onto my chest.

"Yeah. After that little display of non-platonic affection, I either need to jump my husband or have a cold shower."

"You're full of it," I say, shaking my head.

"And you're in denial if you're really still going to tell me that you're just friends with him."

"I am . . . we are . . ." I quickly retort.

"Maybe you'll try to be, but he's definitely not aboard the same 'just friends' train."

"I hate you."

"You love me."

"Maybe," I reply with a huge grin.

"Definitely."

And damn her, now she's watered the seed I long ago buried when it came to liking Thomas, my mind, stomach—and definitely my vagina—won't let me forget about it.

Shit!

6

Thomas

A week later I'm pulling into Cade and Abi's driveway after a day of working from home. Knocking twice and waiting—with no reply—I do what I'm known for, opening the door and making my way inside.

Entering the living room, I look through to the kitchen and stop short when I see Abi's back touching the dining table, Cade's body bent over her and the two of them too busy making out to hear my arrival. Thankfully, they're fully clothed this time.

"Don't mind me. Just let me grab some popcorn to have while watching the show."

They both stop eating each other's faces and as if in slow motion, turn their heads to look at me. Abi's eyes dance with amusement while Cade's narrow in frustration if the growl that follows is anything to go by.

"I'd say I was sorry, but the look on Cade's face is totally worth it."

"Fucker," he mutters as he stands up and pulls his wife back up to standing.

"You love it." I grin and walk over toward them, dipping my head to kiss Abi's cheek.

I give Cade's shoulder a squeeze then make my way into the kitchen to grab myself a beer.

"Help yourself, why don't you?" Cade muses.

"Your casa is my casa."

"So it seems."

It's when I'm walking back toward the living room when Abi steps in front of me, stopping me in my tracks.

"So . . ." she says slowly, a wry smile playing on her lips. "I hear that you've been visiting Amy and Brody a *lot* . . ." She looks up at me expectantly, obviously waiting for a reaction.

Lifting the beer bottle up to my mouth, I take a long, measured pull, studying her while I do it.

"Yeah . . ." I reply, waiting to hear what's going to come next. Whatever it is—and knowing Abi—it'll either be funny as hell, informative, or it's going to piss me off to no end.

She makes a little growl in the back of her throat and grabs my hand, tugging—no *dragging*—me into the living room before dropping onto the couch and pulling me down to sit beside her.

My head snaps to Cade, my eyes begging for a rescue. However, instead of stepping up like any best friend should, he just grins and shakes his head.

"I'll go order us some dinner. Abi's off to Amy's for some *Bachelor* auction thing."

"It's the first episode of the new *Bachelor* season. It's a *very* important event in my social calendar," she retorts rather empathically.

"Don't know why you need to watch that when you've got such a fine specimen of a man at your disposal right here," Cade announces from the kitchen.

"Just you wait, Doctor Hottie. You get to reap all the benefits every week when I get home."

"Oh jeez, Carsen. Married for a few months and *already* you're down to weekly. I did warn you not to let her eat the abstinence—I mean, *wedding*—cake."

Abi's hand darts out and whacks my bicep. "Shut it you. If anything, he gets laid *more* now than before he took me off the market."

Cade bursts out laughing. "I took *you* off the market. Right," he scoffs.

Abi shoots narrowed eyes his way. "You watch it, buddy, or else weekly will become a fantasy."

"Don't make threats you can't deliver on, Spitfire."

"Bite me."

"If you insist . . ."

"Will you two get a room, already," I reply with a grin.

"We do. We have several, in fact. The living room, the dining room, the bathroom . . ." Cade calls out.

"I think I need to throw up," I mutter.

"Don't be jealous of our sexathon. At least we waited until after you'd moved out," Abi says with a shrug.

I spear her with a look. "Do you forget the kitchen incident?"

"Oh, yeah," she giggles, her eyes looking over my shoulder toward her husband. "That was fun. We should definitely do *that* again."

It's then her expression changes, her mood going from fun to all business in the blink of an eye.

"What are your intentions with my friend?" Abi asks, her face dead serious and very 'un-Abi' like.

I purse my lips to hold back laughter, losing the fight the moment she narrows her eyes.

"I'm serious, Thomas. Amy likes to show the world she's strong and independent, but she has a soft spot for charming men who say all the right words and do all the right things at the right time."

I tilt my head and study her. "You're saying I'm charming?" I reply with a huge grin.

She whacks my arm again. "You know you are. I've seen you pull at the club before. You bat your lashes better than a Southern debutante."

"So you're telling me I flirt like a woman?" I reply, deadpan.

"Gah!" she growls, balling her hands into fists. "Seriously, Thomas. Why are you still visiting my best friend? Why the secret, covert visits when the rest of us aren't there?"

"They weren't—"

"Right," she scoffs. "That's why no one knew about them until yesterday when Mia asked Amy what you were doing in her kitchen doing *dishes*."

I chuckle and watch her lips thin as I take the opportunity to partake in one of my favorite pastimes of late, riling up Abi.

"I *was* doing the dishes," I muse. "I was also cleaning the kitchen counter, if that matters."

Cade sputters from the doorway and Abi's angry eyes snap to her husband. "Not helping, Cade."

"You're adorable," he says.

"And *you're* not getting any when I get home."

"Let's see how that works out for you, Spitfire. One look at my cock and you'll be riding me like a dog in heat. Especially after watching *The Bachelor.*"

"Did you just call me a bit—"

"No. No, I didn't," Cade says, backtracking at lightning speed. "You're beautiful tonight, sweetheart."

"Watch it buddy or else you'll have the pleasure of experiencing blue balls in the form of my knee in your junk *and* from joining your friend here in a long period of abstinence."

"Hey! Don't bring me into this," I muse in mock annoyance.

This brings Abi's attention back to me. "You haven't answered the question, Thomas," she says in a sing-song tone.

"That's because there is no answer, Abi-Jane."

"There's always an answer."

"You want to know why I've been visiting Amy? Because we're friends."

"That's a cop out and you know it."

"How is that a cop out?" I reply with a laugh, wrongly relishing in the fact that I'm frustrating her.

"You've been visiting her every few days since she got home from the hospital. You've been present, helpful and by all accounts, extremely good at cleaning."

Cade snorts and swallows his laughter quickly by taking a swig from his beer when Abi spears him with a glare. When I don't answer, she presses on.

"Look, I just want you to be careful with her."

I study her and decide that honesty is best. This is Abi, one of my closest friends and all she's doing is looking out for Amy. The same thing I've been trying to do.

The difference is that I've wanted to keep my interactions with Amy private, between just the two of us, for no other reason that I feel connected to her. I said I wanted to be here for her and that's exactly what I've been trying to do.

And part of me *likes* that Amy and I have had time away from her friends and my friends because of this exact situation.

Mia was suspicious yesterday and obviously grilled Amy before passing on the gathered intel to Abi and now I just *know* that the pressure is going to go on us. I don't want that. I want to spend more time getting to know Amy because everything I've seen so far has me wanting more and that's not something I've experienced for a *long* time.

"You really want to know?" I ask, knowing the answer already.

"Yes," she replies sounding exasperated.

"I'm just being there for her. Being a friend."

"Amy already has friends."

"And now she has one more," I reply with a smirk.

"And you're doing that by *cleaning* for her?"

"Yep. I make snacks and cups of tea too," I continue, a wry smile playing on my lips.

"And the secrecy?"

"So that my nosey friends don't get ideas and start interfering."

"You know that ship has sailed now, right?" Cade pipes up, walking across the room and sitting down in the leather recliner before grabbing the remote and turning on the television.

"Probably."

"She has a baby, Thomas."

"Funnily enough I know that, given that I helped deliver him."

"You've gotta tread carefully," she says.

"I know this and I want you to know, I've. Got. This."

She opens her mouth to say something else but snaps it shut, instead choosing to study me, her eyes scanning my face as if looking for any sign of insincerity.

"Okay then," she says, standing up and tilting her head down. "You've got this. But if you hurt her, I'll cut your dick off." I choke on my beer as she ruffles my hair with her fingers then moves to her husband, dipping down to kiss him.

"Right, I'm off to get my *Bachelor* fix. I'll say hi to Amy for you, Thomas," she says in a saccharine sweet voice.

"Spitfire . . ." Cade muses, meeting her eyes and communicating some unspoken command.

"You're so no fun. That wedding ring should come with a warning. Upon use, your previously footloose and fancy-free boyfriend will turn into a spoil sport husband." She scoots back as she says it, making sure she's out of Cade's reach before poking her tongue out at him.

"Bye, boys," she adds before grabbing her purse from the coffee table and disappearing through the front door.

Thomas: How's the bachelor thing going?

Amy: Normal people say hi when they text.

Thomas: Hi

Amy: Hi back

I wait for a while, expecting another message to come through. When it doesn't, I almost second guess whether to text her again.

Thomas: So the bachelor thing?

Amy: Did you really text me to ask about that? I know Abi gave you the third degree.

Amy: If it helps, all of the girls grilled me when they arrived. It seems that the phone tree in the group is extremely effective.

Thomas: I just thought I'd text to say Hi and see how your day was. Was it the doctor's visit today?

Amy: It's scary how you remember these things.

Thomas: Call it a talent of mine.

Amy: You mean you have talents other than being my man slave?

Thomas: Man-slaves walk around in loincloths and nothing else. I don't own one, but if you insist . . .

Amy: I just spat tea all over the floor because of you. Now I'm getting weird looks.

Thomas: If you had a man slave there, he could take care of the mess.

Amy: How does one get a man slave? Is there a 1–800-loincloths-R-us?

Thomas: If there's not, there should be.

Amy: What about an apron? Will that do in lieu of a loincloth?

Thomas: It's hard to get good working conditions these days.

Amy: Is there a slave union?

Thomas: I should look into it.

Amy: You do that. They can advise me if the working conditions I am providing are substandard. But yes, six week check with doctor today. I'm officially all healthy, healed and ready to go.

I shouldn't have read that text mid-swallow. Deciding it's

safer to avoid all talk of what exactly she's ready for, I change the topic.

Thomas: How was Brody today?

"You have a goofy grin on your face," Cade says, breaking my concentration. "And your phone is vibrating more than my wife's bedside drawer."

"I've told you more than once, Carsen. If you're not up to the job, I'm more than happy to step in and show Abi what being with a r*eal* man is like."

"It seems that you've already got your hands full with your own woman."

Before I can stop myself, my head snaps up to find him arching a brow my way.

For a man who's not easily embarrassed, the heat I feel in my cheeks is almost a new experience for me. Thankfully, he lets it go, switching to his default 'give Thomas shit' mode.

"Who are ya texting?" he says in a dumbass, teenage jock-like voice.

"Uh . . . dude . . . it's this chick I know," I mimic back.

"Is she hot?"

"Smoking," I reply, sounding just like Keanu Reeves in *Bill & Ted's Excellent Adventure.*

"You gonna go for third base with her?"

"Nah. She's one of those good girl types, hand holding and nothing more."

"Duuuuude . . ." he says slowly, his lips twitching.

I stop fighting my grin and shake my head at him. "It's just Amz. I was just checking in with her."

"Just Amz?" His shit-eating smirk matches his teasing tone.

"Shut it." I can't stop myself from grinning back at him.

My phone vibrates, capturing my attention. Swiping the message open, I'm met with a photo of a sleeping Brody sucking his thumb. It's the cutest thing I've ever seen.

"You've got it bad, dude."

"Dude or 'duuuuude,'" I shoot back.

"Stop deflecting. Is there more to this Amy thing than just you being there for them?"

"Honestly?" I ask, meeting his eyes.

"Yep."

"Maybe," I reply.

"Are you going to do something about it?"

"She's got a lot on her plate. I'm fine with things as they are now." I know it's a lie, but until I know whether I even have a shot with her, I'm not going to lay myself out for anyone, even Cade.

"So you're friend-zoning yourself?"

"I'm so far entrenched in the friend zone, I'm almost sure I've created a new dictatorial state."

"Wouldn't take much to immigrate to the 'not-friend zone,'" he adds with a smirk.

This is a double brow lift moment. "Dr. Cade Carsen, Emergency medicine specialist, self-orphaned son of Cade and Annabel Carsen, husband, golf pro, and matchmaker? You need to update your resume."

"You're a dick," he says, throwing a beer cap my way.

"And you're a vagina."

"I'm happy with that. They're tough and strong and can take a good pounding when asked."

I chuckle and shake my head. "Just don't let the girls railroad you into anything. Take it at your own pace."

"Yes, Dad."

"Not yet but hopefully soon," he murmurs, returning his attention to the game.

My eyes go wide but I don't say anything because although I knew that Abi and Cade would start a family in the future, for some reason the reality that this would happen—and seemingly soon—brought to the surface all my feelings of inadequacy.

To distract myself, and redirect my thoughts, I return my attention to my phone.

Thomas: You want a visitor on Thursday night?

Amy: You don't have to, Thomas. I can clean my own house lol

Thomas: I know I don't have to but I want to and I like helping you out around the house. Gives you time to focus on Brody.

Amy: You're a nice guy, you know that?

Thomas: Shh don't tell anyone, you'll ruin my street cred.

Amy: Your secret's safe with me.

Thomas: See you Thursday, I'll bring takeout.

Amy: Sounds good. Have a good night.

Thomas: Enjoy your bachelor fantasy

Amy: Abi and Mia got all the good ones, but I fared all right. Who won the game?

I glance up at the screen then back down to my phone.

Thomas: Bears are leading by 14.

Amy: Such a shame. Although I know the Broncos will kick their ass in a few weeks

Those are fighting words.

Thomas: And with that, this Bears' fan bows out. Your father and son would be ashamed of you.

Amy: The girls are eyeing me up wondering why I'm giggling.

Thomas: Tell them a hot sexy man slave sans loincloth is demanding your attention.

Amy: Lmao. Will do. See you Thursday.

And with that, I return my attention back to the game, the beer in my hand, my smart-ass best friend, and looking forward to takeout with Amy in a few days' time.

7

Amy

The girls had ganged up on me the minute they all arrived on Monday night, wanting to know everything there was to know about Thomas's visits; how often, since when, and how it all came about.

My explanation of "he wants to be there for me and Brody" didn't seem to go over well but when they realized there was nothing more to it, they let it go.

Well, for the moment anyway. But in all honesty, that is all there is to it, no matter how much I wish things might be different.

I'd like to think we've built a good friendship out of it and Brody loves having him around; even if he's barely awake long enough to see him most of the time.

Now it's Thursday afternoon and would you believe it, in the time I have to myself while Brody is sleeping, all I can think about is why Thomas might feel the need to help me.

I'm not dumb enough to say no. I'm a single, first-time mom with an almost seven-week-old son who is thankfully a fantastic sleeper—for now, anyway—but who's also very time-consuming for a little guy.

Thomas has surprised me. He's nothing like the cocky playboy I'd pegged him for.

There have been moments of whoosh, instances of stomach flips, and the introduction of a whole new level of comfort with him I never thought was possible.

"So . . ." I say after eating *way* too much food. "How did you know I was a shrimp and chicken kind of girl?" I turn on the couch and fold my legs up under my body, getting comfortable.

He shoots me a wry smirk. "I have my ways."

"And are those ways called Abi and Mia?"

"Maybe . . ." he replies, and unless I'm seeing things, he almost looks bashful.

"Definitely Abi. We used to have Takeout Thursdays before Brody arrived."

"Why not now?" he asks, spooning some noodles into his mouth.

I watch the cords in his throat move, his jaw tensing and relaxing, and I swear my eyes glaze over a little.

Buck up, Amz. Remember, STD, abstinence, baby . . .

I've got no time for men. Even if he is really nice, like in a 'I need to jump you and ride you like a merry-go-round' kind of way.

I shake my head to clear my goofy haze and shrug, picking up my cup of tea and cradling it between my hands.

"She's busy, I'm *really* busy . . . I don't know, it's just life I guess. We're all growing up and moving on."

His brows furrow and his expression turns contemplative

before he schools his features and smiles. "Maybe we should restart this tradition. Just the Thomas and Amy version."

Thankfully I'd just swallowed my mouthful because I kind of laugh/snort in the most unladylike way.

"You want to start Thomas Takeout Thursdays?"

He shrugs and grins. "It is rather catchy, don't ya think?" he says, his lips twitching with amusement.

"There would need to be rules and a firm understanding of everything the tradition entails," I say, secretly loving the carefree and wonderfully easy banter we've got going. It's like I'm seeing a whole new side of this man, Brody's birth seemingly being the catalyst for whatever change has been made to our friendship.

I'm the first to admit that my out of control—and still not back to normal—hormones are having a field day with all this Thomas time. He's funny, charming, yet so down to earth and thoughtful.

"Do you want to stay and watch a movie? I mean, you don't have to, and don't feel obligated to stay or anything, I just thought maybe, if you didn't have any other plans, that you might want to."

Shit. Fudge. Damn. Way to sound like a babbling idiot, Amz.

His eyes are warm and one side of his mouth is tipped up, his one dangerous dimple out and proud and firmly engaged.

"Depends . . ." he says slowly while making his way toward my entertainment center.

Okay, I'll play. "Depends on?"

He crouches down in front of the DVD rack and runs his thumb down the titles. "Mmm?"

Deciding this could take a while, I sit down on the edge of

my couch as he scans the movies before making a selection, trying hard to drag my eyes away from his perfect round ass.

Looking over his shoulder, he catches me mid-ass peek, his lips curling up into a knowing grin. Thankfully, he doesn't call me out on it because that would be mortifying and might result in me locking myself in Brody's room until I knew Thomas had left.

"You're a Marvel fan," he says, pulling out a DVD before straightening and turning toward me.

"I'm an anything superhero, superhuman, or hot guys in spandex fan."

"Good to know," he muses, holding out Thor and quirking a brow. "And will an Asgard prince do for your viewing pleasure tonight?"

"I'm more of a Loki fan myself, but if you're Team Thor, don't let me stop you." I wave my hand out to the TV and DVD player and soon he's sitting down at his end of the couch as the opening credits play in the background.

Um, since when did Thomas have an end of anything in my house?

I don't know why but as soon as he sits down and I do what I normally do when I'm laxing out watching a movie, my entire body tenses. In fact I freeze when it hits me that I'm sitting on a couch, in my living room, watching a movie with Thomas. This is weird, right?

This man has seen my vagina and it wasn't even good for me. Yet, he's here, he bought me shrimp fried rice and kung-pao chicken and now he's watching a DVD with me, on my couch.

He's not cleaning, he's not here to help me out. He bought takeout and is now slouching back on my couch, shoes off, ankles crossed, watching the screen like it's the most riveting movie on earth.

It's a good ten minutes into the movie when it happens.

"Sweetness, it's a movie not a torture session. Get your ass over here."

"What?" I gasp, my eyes bugging out of my head as I turn to look at him.

"You're all tense and curled up in a ball over there. Unless I smell, come over here, I'm a cuddler and I'm cold. So I figure I can kill two birds with one Amy and get my cuddle fix while we watch the movie."

Ah, hello? Universe? It's Amy calling. Are you punking me?

It's not like I can say no right now, not that I want to. I mean, he's Thomas.

He's been a rock for Brody and I since my rather impromptu birth. And *not* in a 'he's only doing this to get in my pants' way which, to be honest, I would've probably expected had I not gotten to know the real man behind the cocky clown exterior.

We talk, we laugh, we've shared milestone moments together when Brody has done random things like his first six-hour sleep at night (I texted him randomly at two a.m. to tell him) and it was Thomas who got the gift of Brody's first smile at four weeks old.

For a single thirty-five-year-old guy, Thomas has given up a *lot* of potential socializing time to help me out. He wants to cuddle me, who am I to say no?

Doesn't mean I'm above making him work for it a little, or at least squirm.

"Oh," I say, slipping into the role of the perfect hostess and standing up from the couch. "I'll turn up the heat—"

I don't get the rest of the word out because I'm hooked around the waist by a strong forearm and pulled back down into Thomas's lap, shrieking as I go. Yes, I said his *lap* before I can protest, I'm shifted to the side so my ass is on the couch, my legs are draped over his, and my chest is plastered to his side.

My head snaps to his and his dancing eyes meet my wide-eyed expression, my mouth dropped open like a fly catcher. "Don't need the heat up when you're right here."

Okay that makes me blush and I narrow my eyes at him, wondering what his game is.

"Thomas, I'm not—" I'm stopped when his hands move to my bare feet, his fingers deliciously kneading my soles.

"You've been busy all day and as much as you try to hide it, I know you're tired and I want to give you a foot rub."

"You don't have . . . to . . ." I reply, my cheeks heating as my voice turns breathy.

"Amz, relax. Let me do something for you for a change."

"You *have* been doing stuff for me since Brody was born," I explain.

"This is adult time. Everything else has been helping out with Brody, and I'll keep doing *that* as long as you need me to."

"But I—"

"Or want me to." That shuts me up and in the silence that follows, his body heat seeps into me and I decide that resistance is probably futile and crazy. I mean, it's Thomas and he doesn't do anything he doesn't want to do. He never has for as long as I've known him and I doubt that'll ever change.

Fuck it, if he wants to rub my feet while we watch a movie, so be it. I'd be a fool to say no when his hands are working miracles against my skin. Men are weird and Thomas might have a foot fetish for all I know. Who am I to judge?

"Everything set for the christening this weekend?" he says softly, like it's a normal everyday occurrence to give me a foot rub and have a casual chat.

"I'm starting to see how you do so well sorting businesses out."

He chuckles but doesn't stop his *almost* orgasm-inducing foot rub. "Why's that?"

I nod to my feet, trying not to moan like a wanton hussy as he digs his thumbs in. "If you want something, you make it happen."

"You have no idea," he murmurs but by the time his words register in my head there's a loud crash from the TV and—in my mind at least—the moment is gone.

And as I decide to let that particular comment go and instead focus on the movie, I relax my body and let myself enjoy the moment, however fleeting it may be.

I open my eyes to be met by a blank-screen television and a warm soft—but *hard*—body beneath me. *Oh shit.*

Brody's frustrated grunts and gahs come over the baby monitor on the coffee table and I throw my hand out to quickly turn down the sound so I don't wake my unintentional mattress.

Stamping down the freak out fighting inside of me, I gently

ease myself off him, freezing when his hand on my hip drifts down to my ass and tenses.

My eyes snap to his, a silent sigh of relief escaping me when I see he's still asleep.

Having to face him right now would *definitely* cause me to lose the tight hold I have on my mortification.

The last thing I remember is cuddling into him—at his insistence—and despite being tense at the start, I soon melted into his side as his warmth seeped into me.

He didn't try anything, he wasn't angling for a grope or even looking to start something. It seems he genuinely just wanted to snuggle down and watch the movie.

But that was hours ago, and now I'm disengaging my body from his, to get to my baby boy in the next room.

Don't get me wrong, I'm not saying I haven't imagined—read: fantasized about—getting close to Thomas, beside him, on top of him, beneath him . . . but where both parties are willing and *awake.*

Once I'm free and standing beside the sofa, I check one last time to make sure I haven't disturbed him before quietly leaving the room and down the hall to my son's room.

"Hey, baby," I coo when I reach his crib, reaching down and lifting him up to bring him to my chest. "You saved Mommy from doing something stupid."

Of course he says nothing but as I move to my nursing chair in the corner of his room, part of me wishes he'd miraculously become a baby genius and say "you can thank me later, Mama."

Getting comfortable, I gently rock him while he assumes his position and helps himself to the never ending milk bar.

Stroking his head as he feeds, I can't stop thinking about how and *where* I woke up moments ago.

"Mommy doesn't know what she's doing," I say quietly. My voice the only sound in the room. "You saved me from a world of embarrassment. Maybe a possible bad decision too."

I sigh, remembering back to how nice the night with Thomas was. How easy it is to be around him, how different he is to my original impression all those months ago.

"I'm so far in the friend-zone, I've got my own area code. Takeout and movies and he didn't even try to cop a feel. No twitchy fingers, no wandering hands, no sexy eyes hinting at more. I mean, I didn't *think* I wanted a man in my life other than you but sometimes a mommy doesn't mind some male attention."

"I've still got it, don't I? I've got boobs, hips, and ass. My face isn't paper bag worthy, why *wouldn't* he make a pass at me. Unless he doesn't like me like that." Then, like the messed up hormonal mess I am, I try to reason with myself. "But he did try and come on to me when I was pregnant, surely that means something, right?" Brody looks up at me and smiles around my nipple, like what I said was the funniest thing in the world.

"At least you woke me up and saved me a whole lot of awkward. I think I maybe drooled on his chest. How sexy is that? All he did was come over for dinner and he ends up being my mattress. God, I'm a hot mess. Lucky you love me, right baby?"

I hum to Brody while I rock my legs back and forth, watching as his whole body melts into me, totally milk drunk and adorably sleepy.

Fifteen minutes later, I tip toe out of his room after settling him back in his bed, making my way out to the living room where I find the TV turned off and Thomas nowhere to be seen.

If I didn't remember *every* part of his body I was lying on top of and how good it felt, I'd think I had dreamed it all.

It's not until I check my door is locked that I see a note written on the little magnetic whiteboard stuck to my fridge.

Sweetness, thanks for the Chinese, conversation, and cuddles. Next time, you choose the movie but no more superheroes. They give me a complex and make me feel totally inadequate as a man. Thomas Takeout Thursdays are now our thing. So see you next Thursday. P.S. Actually, I'll see you next Saturday afternoon but I couldn't resist saying it.

Snorting with laughter, I'm still grinning, even when I get into bed.

One thing is for sure, any disappointment at finding Thomas gone faded away the moment I saw that note on the wall and now, I'm definitely looking forward to our next TTT.

8

Thomas

It's not eavesdropping if you hear over the baby monitor, right? Because I heard every word that Amy said to Brody last night when she thought I was still asleep.

I probably should've turned it down or left. Maybe drowned the speaker in water to remove any and all temptation to hear what she thought of me—of the potential of *us*—but . . .

I couldn't. I mean, who would?

I'm a curious guy, always have been and probably always will be and there's something to be said about hearing the woman you're potentially interested in express her feelings like that.

I heard Brody over the monitor at least a minute before Amy woke up. After remembering where I was, I focused on more pleasant sensations, like how fucking great it felt to have a woman in my arms. No, it was good to have *Amy* lying on me, chest to chest, legs tangled with mine, her warm soft body melding against my hard one.

I thought she was beautiful before she had Brody, but now she's off the charts hot. Those curves, her eyes, and her dark auburn hair that shines so bright I have to stop myself from touching it. Her smile, her attitude, her infectious energy and total commitment to her son, all of it is amazing.

So yeah, guilty as charged, I heard her talking to Brody when she thought she was alone and let every word sink in. When I knew she was finishing up I decided to save her the awkward turtle moment and leave. She felt embarrassed enough and there was no way I wanted to make her uncomfortable. But I made sure to leave her a note, one that hopefully made up for my hasty departure and also put a smile on her face.

For the first time since I made my vow to Cade, I find myself wanting to spend time with Amy like last night, when I'm there just for her; to spend time with her, talk to her, rile her up and smirk when she scrunches her nose up in frustration. The old me might have been freaked out by the fact that Amy has a child but it's different because it's Brody. That little guy and I had a bond the minute we locked eyes in the cereal aisle. I've got his back, he'll have mine when I'm old and gray. Wait . . . did I honestly just go there?

But now, I'm on a mission. I'm playing the long game but first, I need help and Mia is first on the list.

With the first step in my plan decided on, I pull out of my building's parking garage and into traffic.

I push a button on my steering wheel and activate my phone's Bluetooth.

"Call Mia," I say to the car at large, pulling to a stop in the daily traffic jam that is now an integral—even if annoying—part of my morning routine.

"You do know it's like eight a.m. right?" Mia says by way of greeting. "At least my *husband* knows how to wake me up right," she grumbles, making me chuckle.

"Morning to you too, sunshine."

"Thomas, unless you got laid, hurt, or at the very least maimed, you better have a good reason for calling me so early."

"You have a daughter. I figured you'd be awake."

"Yes I do and she's sound asleep in the bed beside me. Matt carried her in once he'd finished his husbandly chores."

"I doubt it's a chore for him, Meems," I muse.

"You'd be right. Never known him to turn down breakfast à la Mia when it's offered."

"And *this* conversation just went weird," I mutter as Mia's giggle fills the cab.

"So do tell me Mister hot cleaning man, how can I be of service?"

"Do you know what kind of clothes Amy likes?"

"What, are you going to do her laundry now too?"

"No," I reply a bit too quickly. "I need you to buy her an outfit."

I hear a muted girly shriek over the phone and a rustling of sheets, then what sounds like a door closing.

"Why . . . ?" Her voice is almost a shrill, an over excited, far too telling one.

"Sounds like you've *realized* why, Meems."

"You're asking her out?"

"Yes, but it needs to be done right. I want her to be comfortable and ready. She needs to *want* to go out with me, not feel she's doing it out of obligation."

"You're not going to have any problems there," she mutters but I hear every word.

"Say it again?"

"Never mind," she replies quickly before changing the subject. "So where, when, level of dress, just the outside or are we talking the whole shebang?"

"Top to toe and everything in between. I don't want her having to worry about anything, and I mean anything, Mia. Whatever she needs is whatever you'll buy. Just make sure she feels as beautiful as I see her."

"Oooh, you're totally giving her the pretty woman treatment aren't you."

"I'm going to give her everything she deserves. Do you think you can come by my office to grab my credit card?"

"Major swoon alert, Thomas. If I wasn't happily married I might just take a walk on the abstinence-ending side."

"Very funny, Meems."

"You're a catch and I'm liking the idea of you with my best friend the more I think about it. You're a good guy, Thomas Caldwell, cocky attitude notwithstanding."

"Good to know," I muse wryly, "considering who you're married to."

"He's a lucky man. He's also lucky he knows it and shows me every day," she says and I can hear the happiness in her voice. "Now, when do you need all of this done by?"

"Two weeks. Will that give you long enough?"

"I'd get it done in a day if it meant Amy gets some."

"Mia . . ." I warn.

"Sorry, sorry. I'm getting ahead of myself."

"Let's see if she actually *wants* to go out with me first, shall we?"

"You really don't see it, do you?" she says bizarrely.

"See what?"

"Never mind. You men are all the same. Anyway, text me your address. I've never been to your office so I'm going to need directions."

"Will do."

"Cool. Let me get Emma fed and dressed and we'll see you in a few hours. We can talk more then."

"Mia . . ."

"Bye, Thomas," she says cheerfully before ending the call.

"Eyes on the prize, Caldwell," I say to myself, knowing that I'll probably get the same grilling from Mia that I had from Abi but as long as Mia can do what I need her to do, I'll take whatever she dishes up.

We've had two more takeout Thursdays, and watched two more superhero movies—she wasn't kidding about being a Marvel fan—and I've found myself looking forward to each one more than the last.

Nothing has been said about falling asleep together on the couch but there's no way either of us have forgotten about it. I've seen Amy studying me when she doesn't think I'm looking and I've been unapologetic the times she has caught me doing the same. But it hasn't gone any further than that.

I've still got my game plan in play and Mia rang me just yesterday to update me on her progress with her allotted tasks.

Today is Brody's christening though, so definitely not the day to do anything other than play the role of friend. It's made easier by the fact that this whole 'friend zone' situation has an expiry date because I've decided that next Thursday is going to go a hell of a lot different than those that have gone before.

There's just one last piece of the puzzle to fall into place and it will be game on.

And from my baby monitor eavesdropping, I know exactly how to make the first move, one that will leave her with no doubt as to where my feelings lie.

In fact, I'm not going to give her the option of saying no because the one thing that my year of abstinence has taught me it's that hard work is always rewarded. So far it's been in business, this time, it's going to be making sure I look after Amy and Brody in all the ways a man can.

After the ceremony at the church where both Abi and Sean stood up as godparents for Brody, we all gather back at Noah and Zoe's place for lunch.

A few hours later after we've eaten and put the younger kids down for a nap, I change into my swim shorts before diving into the pool.

Having donned swim shorts, and wearing out the older kids in the pool by becoming the Uncle Thomas water playground that throws and dunks and throws again, I spot Zoe, Mia, Abi and Amy lying out on sun loungers and make my move.

Deciding they might also be hot, and in need of some water, I do what any good man would do. Quietly exiting the pool, I grab my towel on the way before shaking my head, throwing drops of water all over them.

"Thomas, you got my shirt wet," Zoe shrieks.

"You're not the only one," Amy mumbles under her breath and my ears prick up. I definitely don't miss the way her eyes hone in on my chest, legs and everything in between.

"Heard that," Mia muses, making my lips twitch. Amy blushes and I cover my mouth to hide my laughter.

"Bitch," Amy hisses, poking her tongue out.

"Caldwell, did you get my wife wet?" Noah says from across the backyard.

"That's what she said," I retort, turning his way.

"He did get me wet," Zoe says with a giggle. "But in my defense, I'm sure I heard Amy say she was wet too." I don't even try to hide my chuckle this time.

"Why are we talking about people getting wet?" Mac asks, walking through the French doors leading out from the kitchen.

"You don't want to know," Sam says, an uncharacteristic wry smile playing on her lips as she pulls up a chair and sits with the girls.

"If it's enough to make Sam smile like that, I do wanna know," Mac replies, sidling up to Daniel who's standing with the rest of the guys.

I hook my towel around my neck and rush her, plastering my damp chest to hers.

"Thomas," she shrieks. "Now I'm dripping," and the whole group laughs, Daniel grinning down at his wife after he pulls her away from me.

"You totally walked into that one, gorgeous."

She makes a harrumph sound which is equally hilarious.

"My job here is done," I say proudly before throwing Mac a smile. Turning around, I make my way over to where Amy is lying down on the sun lounger, shooting her a wink and earning a gorgeous smile, one I wouldn't mind seeing again and again.

It's then a whimper comes out over the baby monitor, one I

recognize as Brody straight away. She starts to move but I put my hand on her shoulder to stop her. "You don't have to, Thom—"

She stops talking when I give her the 'what did I say' look, biting her lip adorably and invoking images in my head of all the other ways I could make her look like that. And right on inappropriate cue, my dick decides to twitch to attention.

I'm abstinent not a monk, and my dick may hate me for my life choices but he's not adverse to making his presence known, like right now.

Wrapping my towel around my waist, I move across the backyard and into the house, ducking into the downstairs bathroom and getting changed back into my clothes before making my way upstairs.

I walk into Noah's son's bedroom where Amy set up Brody's Pack 'n Play when we arrived. Peering over the side, I meet a pair of big and extremely curious hazel eyes.

"Hey buddy, have a good nap?" I ask him as I lift him in up into my arms and cradle him into my chest the way he likes. When he doesn't answer—because seriously, babies are rather selfish in the conversation stakes I've discovered—I continue chatting as I scan the room for his diaper bag, and move it toward the change table set up in the corner of the room.

"Well, we've been having an awesome time while you've been sleeping. You should really work on this overwhelming need for a nap. You missed out on playing in the pool with me and the other kids. You would've loved it too. It's just like a giant bath tub with loads of water."

I undo the snaps of his onesie and like the pro that I now am, have the dirty diaper undone, and his pee missile covered for my protection in the blink of an eye.

"Then I shook my head like a shaggy dog all over the mommies—well, Abi's not a mommy but I bet Uncle Cade will get one past the goal sooner or later—and they shrieked like a bunch of girls before you saved me by waking up. So good on ya, buddy, I owe you one."

A quick twist of the wrist and a flick of my fingers and he's changed, re-snapped, and cradled back into my arm. Then I do what any normal man would do, rolling his dirty diaper into a ball and announcing, "He shoots, he's scooooores," when I make the cool electric bin shot on my first attempt.

"Should we go downstairs now?" I ask him, reaching my spare hand out and opening the bedroom door. "Because the way you're trying to bury your face in my chest tells me you're starving and wanting milk and sorry to say, little dude, I'm totally the wrong person to be expecting anything to eat from."

I know something's up the moment I step out into the backyard with Brody because everyone—and I mean kids included—are watching me with variations of shock, surprise, and amusement on their faces.

"What?" I ask just before they all burst out laughing. All except Amy whose eyes are warm—one could almost say heated—as she watches me walk toward her.

"Ah, hey," I say, somewhat self-consciously, wishing I knew what the hell was going on.

"Do I have something on my face?" I say quietly when I reach her and hand the baby over.

Now it's her turn for her lips to twitch. "Let's just say that you say the cutest of things to my son while changing his diaper." She manages to get that out before letting out a giggle as she kisses Brody's head.

"What do you—" I ask cutting myself off when it hits me, my head snapping up to meet my friends' amused grins.

"Yeah, buddy," Daniel says with a laugh.

"He shoots, he scoooooooores," Cade mocks.

"Fuck," I mutter.

"Thomas!" Amy growls. "Language."

"Shit . . . I mean . . . schnitzel."

"I prefer firetruck," Mia announces with a huge smile.

"Fudge also works well," Zoe adds. "Except maybe when Nate tells his grandmother that Mommy likes fudging with Daddy."

"What?" Abi gasps. "He didn't?"

"Unfortunately he has a mind like a sponge and the mouth of a parrot. So when he very unfortunately heard Mommy say something on the phone to Daddy, he decided it was only fair that he share it with Grandma. Thankfully, she thinks I like baking with her son."

"Um . . ." Noah says, walking up to his wife and squeezing her shoulder, like his personal parrot resting on his shoulders eating a Popsicle of all things. "About that . . ."

Zoe's head snaps around toward her husband. "Oh shi . . . schnitzel. What did you do, Taylor?"

"Mom may have asked me about the fudge we made . . ." His expression turns to a wary one under the intense glare of his wife's narrowed eyes.

"And . . ." Zoe prompts.

"And . . . well . . . I told her I'd never baked a day in my life."

"Dammit . . . I mean . . . donut!" Zoe mutters, shaking her head.

"Donut! Donut! Donut!" her son Nate squeals excitedly from Noah's head.

"Ever noticed that all of your substitute curse words are food, Zoe?" Mia says with a laugh.

Zoe just scowls before reaching up and grabbing Nate. "I want donuts, Mommy," he demands, smooshing his mom's cheeks in his hands, totally forgetting about the Popsicle he was holding. The Popsicle that is now also squashed into Zoe's hair on the side of her head.

"I want a fudge donut. Can we have a fudge donut, Mommy?"

"Go see Aunty Meems, I bet you she knows all about fudge donuts," Zoe says with a grin, dropping her son into her sister's lap with a knowing grin.

"It's Dani that's the donut queen. She told us, remember?" Mia says, making all the women laugh.

"What's that about?" I ask Amy under my breath as I sit down in the chair beside her where she's nursing a now very happy Brody.

She grins at me and shakes her head. "You really don't want to know about that conversation. Believe me."

"You saying that tells me I really do."

"Think about what this group is like, what your friends do with their wives, and then tell me if you want to know what fudge and donuts and Dani knowing all about them, means."

It takes only a few seconds for everything to click in place. "Oh, fuck no."

Amy giggles, leaning into my side like it's the most natural thing in the world. It's only when she freezes and a little 'shit' escapes her lips that she realizes what she's done.

It's when she goes to move away that I shoot my arm around her shoulders and stop her in place.

"Stay," I say quietly, and it's only when her muscles relax again that I let out the breath I didn't realize I was holding.

"Thomas?" she whispers but I don't answer her, I just give her a gentle squeeze of my fingers before pulling her into my side, making it clear that it's where I want her to be.

And it is.

I just need to make it so it's where she wants to be too.

9

Amy

The next Thursday after Brody's christening and Thomas's weird snuggle maneuver, I'm standing half-dressed in a Nordstrom changing room when Mia drapes yet *another* dress that I could never afford—let alone need—over the top of the door.

"Mia, since when do you need my help buying a dress?" I ask, still confused as to why I'm her real life Barbie doll for the day.

"Because it's a special dress and it has to be right," she announces matter-of-factly.

"Is Matt taking you somewhere? Did I forget your anniversary or something?" I swear it wasn't *that* long ago they got married. Or was it . . .

"No, nothing like that. Can you just hurry up? It's weird yelling through a wall at you. Come show Mama what you're made of."

"I feel weird trying on a dress that *you're* going to wear. I don't understand this at all."

"Yeah, yeah. You've said that already. Just get your butt

out here."

I pop my head out of the changing room to where she's sitting outside waiting for me to model a dress she demanded I try on for her.

"It's shark week. I can't try on clothes when I'm feeling fat and bloated." Quirking a brow, I'm beginning to wonder what drugs she might be on and where I can get some.

"You're the smallest I've seen since you had Emma."

"Look," she says, putting one hand on her hip. "I'm good at hiding the monthly bloat. Just go with it."

"Fine," I huff, taking one last look at the mirror and smoothing my hands down the front of the dress Mia threw in my arms the minute she saw it on the rack.

Granted, this is the third shop she's dragged me into and the sixth dress she's made me try on 'for her.' But I think this is definitely the one. It's a chiffon wrap-around dress that falls down into a floaty skirt that sits about three inches above my knees, the soft dusty pink fabric showing off my newfound curves—thanks, Brody—and hiding the small jiggly pouch I have in my abdomen. To be honest, it's the type of dress I'd love to own, or more aptly, have a *reason* to own.

It's the perfect dress for a date, and I know Mia will look spectacular in it.

I draw back the curtain and step out into the changing room at large, standing flat footed in front of Mia and a sleeping Brody in his stroller. "So?" I ask.

Mia tilts her head and scans me head to toe, a slow smile growing on her lips the more she studies me. "It's perfect," she whispers, sounding almost choked up.

"Meems? Are you all right?"

"It's perfect. It's the most *perfect* dress."

"Meems. . . . What's going on?" I say warily.

She opens her mouth but then snaps it shut, her eyes going from soft and warm to almost shuttered and cagey. *What the fuck is up with that?*

"This dress is the one," she announces and I grin at her.

"It's so swishy," I say, giggling as I sway my hips from side to side.

"And clingy," she adds, taking a step back and scanning me again.

"I bet Matt will love it on you." Her eyes going wide before she blinks and nods.

"Great! Let's go. We've still got lingerie and shoes to buy yet."

"What?" I ask to thin air because in the blink of an eye both Mia and my son have disappeared and I'm left standing in a pretty dress—no a *beautiful* dress—in an empty changing room.

With nothing left to do and obviously needing to go rescue my son from a crazy woman, I shrug and go back behind the curtain. Reverently taking off the perfect pretty pink dress, I cross my fingers that one day I too will have a reason to wear something so beautiful and more so, that I'll have someone worth wearing it for.

Having slept through most of the day's shopping shenanigans, Brody is still wide-eyed and bushy-tailed by the time Thomas arrives for Takeout Thursday. I open the door, my phone hooked between my head and my shoulder as I answer the phone.

"Hey, Dad," I say, sweeping my arm out as Thomas walks through the door, food bags in hand.

"Hey, pumpkin. How's my favorite girl and boy doing?" *God, I love my Dad.*

"We're good. How are you guys?" I say as I study Thomas's ass as he moves into the living room.

He places the takeout bags on the coffee table before dropping to the ground and lying down beside Brody.

"You know us, busy, busy."

I giggle. "Yes, retirement must be *so* hard."

"You watch it, missy, or else I'll sic Kristy onto you."

"That's not much of a warning, Dad. I love her."

His voice goes soft. "We've got that in common then."

"Yep. So, to what do I owe the pleasure of this call?"

"Well, I was wondering if you had any plans for Saturday night."

I frown, walking while talking. "Not at this stage. Why?" I ask, suspiciously.

"Kristy and I were talking and it's time you had a night out, sans baby." My eyes widen and if my father was standing right in front of me, I know my mouth would be gaping. This is the *last* thing I expected him to say.

That's not to say I'm adverse to the idea though because I promised myself before Brody was born that I would always be a mom first and foremost, but I'd also always make time for me.

"Dad, that would be awesome. But I have no plans and it's kinda short notice."

He's quiet for a while, so much so that I'm about to check that he's still on the line when he replies. "I'm sure you'll find something to do."

I watch Thomas and Brody out of the corner of my eye as I contemplate my options. Worst case scenario, I could always go to a movie by myself. Or see if Thomas wanted to do something.

Not a date of course, just as friends. Friends go to movies, or drinks, or dinner . . . wait, that's going into date territory.

Abort. Abort.

"Okay. Sounds good. Brody does a good six-hour stretch at night right now so he'll be asleep most of the time, and I can feed him before I go."

"Yeah, let's not talk about nursing. I may be a down to earth, hip grandpa but I still don't want to think about that. Deal?"

Now that definitely makes me laugh. "Sure. No breast milk talk."

"Amy . . ." he says in his well-practiced 'dad' voice.

"You're so easy to wind up, old man."

"And you're a brat."

"Always have been, always will be," I muse. "Dad, can I call you tomorrow to sort out the details? It's just that Thomas has arrived with dinner and I need to get Brody settled for bed."

"Sure, pumpkin. We'll talk tomorrow. Say hi to Thomas from me." Okay, now *that's* weird.

"Will do. See ya, Dad."

"Bye. And remember, make some plans for Saturday."

"Yes, Dad. Bye," I say before hanging up, a goofy grin on my face. I really got lucky with my dad. When Mom passed away fifteen years ago, Dad had to step up and play the role of both parents, something he totally rocked.

When he met Kristy six years ago, he was worried about

how I'd take it. But Kristy was exactly what Dad needed at that time in his life. For a man who's always given me everything I ever needed and worked his ass off to make sure of it, I was over the moon that he met someone who wanted to do exactly the same thing for him.

Kinda helps that Kristy is awesome too.

"Hey," I say, dropping the phone on the table. "Sorry about that, Dad called just as you arrived."

"No problem. I was just having an enthralling conversation with Brodz here about a new client I met today. Year-long contract, performance bonus, and a real challenge for me. It's going to be *great,* isn't that right, buddy," he says, rubbing his hand on Brody's tummy.

"This is totally turning into a boys' club," I muse, walking past them to grab some plates from the kitchen.

"I can't help it if your son is as irresistible as his mother."

Try as I might to ignore the fluttering butterflies in my stomach, I'm still wearing a goofy grin when I return to the living room.

"Irresistible, huh?" I say, tapping his shoulder with my foot as I pass them on the floor, Thomas lying on his side and Brody lying on his back underneath his activity gym.

Lifting his head up, he shoots me a devilish grin. "Yep. Totally."

"I'm starting to think you only like me for my baby," I tease.

He rolls onto his back and folds his arms behind his head, his eyes locking with mine. "Nah, I have a thing for his mom too."

Alert the media. My ovaries are set to detonate in 3, 2, 1 . . .

Needing a diversion to stop myself from acting on my first instinct which is to jump him then and there, I decide a subject change is in order. "So . . . ready to eat?"

His lips twitch and I know he can see straight through me. Thankfully, he lets it slide and pushes himself up to standing. "It wouldn't be Takeout Thursday if we didn't actually eat."

"Then it would just be a normal Thursday, and I kind of like our new tradition," I say, shooting him a wink and bending down to grab the baby.

"I could've done that for you, you know?"

"Yes, but then I wouldn't have gotten bubba cuddles," I say, burrowing Brody into me.

"I see I'm not the only one who likes cuddling." And as if I could ever forget, I'm reminded of just how good it felt to wake up in Thomas's arms two weeks ago.

I open my mouth but snap it shut again. I mean, what can I say to that?

"Ah yeah," I murmur. Why is he acting weirder than normal? Not weird, per se. Maybe more . . . comfortable. Yes, totally comfortable like he comes to my house every night to lie down on my floor with my son.

Dinner eaten, mindless television on in the background, and I'm giving Brody a last top up of the night before putting him down to bed.

My comfort level around this man continues to surprise me, as does his nonchalance to the fact that I'm sitting here with my boob out, nursing my son. A son that isn't his but amazingly is more his than anyone else's.

It's one of the things that freaks me out about my rapidly growing feelings for Thomas. I don't just have to think about me anymore, I have Brody. He's already connecting with

Thomas—maybe even as much as I am—and it's obvious that Thomas has a bond with him too. Maybe it's that same link that he's forged with me, although ours was born from a shared experience, the bond he has with Brody has been nurtured. And fuck do I love that he wanted to do that.

When Brody is milk drunk enough for my liking, I pull him off, quickly tucking my boob away.

"Let me put him down and you can choose the movie," Thomas says, closer to me than he was before. I nod as he gently slides his arms against me and underneath Brody.

"Say good night, Mommy," Thomas says softly, bending down to lean over the two of us, looking down at my son.

Dipping my head to kiss Brody's cheek, I nuzzle my nose against his temple before one last quick peck on his forehead. It takes everything in me to avoid thinking about how close Thomas is to me right now and acknowledging the heat that I can feel coming from him.

When he lifts the baby up, the scent of his aftershave surrounds me, threatening to send me into an instant orgasm-inducing haze and suddenly I'm penciling in plans to buy it in bulk. Other than the smell of my baby boy's skin and maybe donuts fresh out of the oven, I can't think of anything better.

If it was at all possible, I could definitely fall in love with this man. Part of me is cursing the STD that friend-zoned me all those months ago.

Then the pregnancy bump clam-jammed any chance of anything happening between us.

Oh and his abstinence, that also would've been a thorn in the side of any potential *anything* too.

"I'll be back," he says quietly, moving Brody to his shoulder. "I dare you to choose a movie that isn't superhero or superhuman related," he says with a grin.

"So chick flick it is then," I tease.

"Whatever you want, sweetness." And I watch with no small amount of admiration as he walks my son out of the room and down the hall.

I'm in soooooo much trouble.

It's after watching *The Notebook*—I did warn him he'd have to watch a chick flick—that everything I thought I knew about Thomas and the 'friend-zone' between us is blown to smithereens.

"So," he says, turning toward me on the couch, his knee nudging mine. "When was the last time you were taken out on a date?"

"What do you mean?" I ask, mirroring his position.

"How long has it been since you went out with a man," he says softly, his voice as smooth as melted chocolate. "On a date. Dinner, drinks, conversation, flirting, and the anticipation of potential groping at the end of the night?"

Whoa. Hold up. Did he just say what I think he just said? Surely I've fallen asleep during the movie again and this is a dream.

"Amy?"

Remember when I said I wanted the whoosh? Well, that right there got me a big whoosh, a tidal wave whoosh, possibly between my legs . . . Just to be safe, I clench my Kegels for safe measure.

I take a moment to think about it. The last date I went on

was with a customer from the bar. He seemed nice, good looking, well-dressed with a dazzling smile that had an unspoken promise of wickedness.

Unfortunately for me, it was all for show. He was actually dull as dishwater and in no way as interesting as the first impression led me to believe. When he asked to split the bill, despite wearing a two thousand dollar tailored suit, I was out of there faster than Brody's sperm donor when I told him I was pregnant.

"Maybe a year and a half," I reply on a whisper, my eyes locking with his, trapped in his sexy force field, not ever wanting to escape.

Isn't it amazing how a few months and a very public loss of dignity can change a girl's perspective on life?

"That's a damn shame, sweetness, because you deserve dinner, drinks, good conversation, and flirting."

"What? No groping?" I ask, one hand instinctively going to my hip as I quirk an eyebrow at him.

He leans his body as close as it can be without touching me but God how I wish it were. I remember how warm he was on Sunday at Noah's and there's no way I've forgotten how comfy he is to sleep on.

"A woman like you would get more than groping. But not until at *least* the third or fourth date." He dips his head so he's all I can see, his voice low and gravelly and talking to places on my body I'd almost forgotten existed.

"A hand pressing on your back as you're led into the restaurant, a little-too-long squeeze of your fingers across the table while you wait for your meal, a not-so-innocent brush of a leg against yours, and a gentle brush of the lips against your hand as you're led to your front door, then a soft promising kiss . . ." his lips brush my cheek, his warm breath fanning across my skin, " . . . that leaves you with a slow burning ache that lasts long into the night."

Okay, it's safe to say I've *never* had a date like that or known a man like that who'd ever want to do that with me and to me.

I've also never experienced anything close to the mini-orgasm I may have just had the moment Thomas Caldwell's lips touched my skin.

Damn, he's good.

"Are you asking me out on a date?" I ask.

"I want dinner, drinks, conversation and the potential for groping, yes."

"But how will I—" he cuts me off by pressing his thumb against my lips. Unable to stop myself, I touch my tongue against his skin just to taste him.

"Babysitting? All sorted," he says with a knowing grin and suddenly Dad's phone call makes sense.

Sneaky bastard.

"Something to wear? Sorted." Freaking hell, he even recruited Mia for his mission. No wonder she had me trying on ten million outfits.

"A few hours of pampering at Kate's salon on Saturday afternoon? Also sorted."

Whoosh. Whoosh. Whoosh.

"The only thing that isn't confirmed . . ." he says, leaning into the couch, even *closer* to me, " . . . is whether you actually want to go out on a date with me."

Dinner, drinks, adult conversation and the potential of being groped and having the opportunity to do the same to him?

Um . . . let me think on that . . .

"Let me get this straight. You're really asking *me* out on a date?" My voice squeaks on the word date, my heart, my head, and my lady parts all bracing for him to say 'psych' and ruin all their days. Not giving him a chance to get a word in edgeways, I continue. "You think," I say, my voice shaking, "that I'd say no after you've organized everything for me and already made it the best date I'll ever go on, and it hasn't even happened yet."

Then the funniest—and most adorable—thing happens. The cocky and always-confident man beside me looks almost sheepish.

It's not the first time I've seen this vulnerable, honest side of him but from everything I've heard about him, I think I'm one of the few people he allows to see it.

Then he seals the deal, reaching his hand up to cup my jaw, his thumb sweeping out across my cheek, his eyes trailing the movement before meeting mine.

"I was worried you'd say no." *Mega whoosh, woman down. I'm totally D.O.N.E, done for now.*

I lift my hand to cover his on my face and decide the best way forward is total honesty. So, taking a deep breath, I let him know *exactly* where I stand on the subject.

"Thomas Caldwell, if you thought I'd say no, then you *really* haven't been paying attention."

Then the most gratifying thing happens. He stares at me wide-eyed for merely a second before dropping his head back as he bursts out laughing.

Job well done, Amy. Job well done.

All I have to do now is count down the forty-four hours until Saturday night.

10

Thomas

I'm nervous. Why the hell am I nervous?

I've never been more anxious about anything than I am about tonight.

I've dated—obviously *more* than dated if my medical records are anything to go by—but I haven't been averse to dipping my toe in the proverbial dating pool in the past.

So much is riding on tonight though. I want it to be perfect. It *needs* to be perfect. Amy deserves nothing but the best, and I may not be perfect, but I know I'm going to be the best man for her.

Tonight is about Amy as a woman, not Amy as Brody's mom.

That's why I took charge of every little detail so she wouldn't have anything to worry about. Or maybe it was so that she wouldn't have an excuse to say no.

I'm a goner for Amy and I'm definitely sunk for her son. If I'm feeling this more than she is, I'm going to be the schmuck forced to watch some other man take the place in their lives that should—and hopefully always will be—mine.

Making my move on Amy is not something I've done for shits and grins. I just hope she and everyone else realizes that.

Shit, I'm well and truly fucked if this doesn't pan out between us.

Leaving my car parked at the curb, I make my way up the pathway and through the lobby of her building, taking the stairs to the second floor. I take a moment outside her door to take a slow, calming breath, needing those few seconds to get my game face on because this could be one of the most important nights of my life. It could be the start of something that most men dream about getting their shot at.

Lifting my arm, I knock twice and it takes what seems like a lifetime before I hear the door unlock then sweep open, and with it, every ounce of oxygen left in my lungs.

"Jesus," I spit out the moment I lay my eyes on her.

"What?" she says, looking down her front then back up at me. "Don't tell me Brodz spit up on me."

God, she's cute. She honestly has no clue the effect she has on me.

"You're gonna have to give me a minute, sweetness." I can't tear my eyes away from her. For the first time in a while, I'm speechless. Her dress is stunning, her makeup is flawless and her auburn hair is a sea of curls sweeping down her back. But that's not what has rendered me mute, it's just *her* and it hits me that I'm the luckiest son of a bitch I know.

"Why then?" I don't answer, too lost in fantasies of things I just can't do right now.

"Earth to Thomas. Why do you need a minute?"

"Maybe more than a minute . . ." I fight back the urge to

push her inside and show her exactly how I'm feeling right now.

"Why?" she says, her hand going to her hip, her tone verging on annoyed.

I close the distance between us, one hand covering hers on her hip, my fingers melding with hers, the other I lift up to her face, my eyes entranced as I move a wayward tendril of hair behind her ear. I'm so close now, it's taking everything I have not to take her against the wall and kiss her.

When her vanilla perfume hits me, I know I'm a goner. Dipping my head, I softly press my lips against her cheek, allowing myself that one moment to take her in before I give her the answer she's waiting for.

"Because I already thought you were the most beautiful woman I'd ever met," I whisper, my voice rough and low. "But right now, the vision of you in that dress is making it hard to fucking breathe."

Suddenly without warning, her door is wrenched wide, the space behind her filled by the broad chest of none other than her father.

"Are you hitting on my daughter when her son and I are ten feet away?" he asks, his face thunderous and downright fucking scary.

"Gar—"

Amy steps back and rolls her eyes before turning toward him. "Dad, you think you could at least wait until the end of the date to pull the 'scary father' gag?"

Gareth chuckles and dips down to kiss her temple, saying, "Party pooper," before letting her go. He looks over at me. "You take care of my girl, Thomas."

I reach out and grab Amy's hand, giving her fingers a gentle squeeze. "You've got no worries there."

"No, I don't think I do either," he replies and I struggle to not laugh at Amy's wide eyes and gaping mouth.

"Should I leave you two alone? Maybe you'd like to take my *dad* out instead of me?"

I pull her into my side, wrapping my arm around her shoulders. It's a bold move on a first date but somehow, all of my nerves are gone. This feels more like a fourth date than a first. Her body relaxes into mine and all of this suddenly feels more right than anything I've felt before.

Right and good.

"Now off you go. Don't worry about us. Kristy and I have everything covered."

"Maybe it's not you two I'm worried about," she teases.

"Oh c'mon," Gareth replies, feigning offense, "I've only given Brody one beer so far. That's his limit. He tried to argue but I had to put my foot down."

"Stop!" she says with a laugh. "I'm allowed to be the overprotective mom. It's part of the job description."

"Just as it's my job as your father to make sure you get out there and have some fun before Brody's old enough to drive you crazy and cause gray hair." He turns to me. "Take her away already before she decides to barricade herself in my grandson's room."

"I wouldn't do that," she gasps, slowly and totally not inconspicuously edging back into the apartment.

Gareth quirks a brow and she quickly shuts her mouth, stopping in place. "Right. See, you were thinking about it. Have a good night, *kids,* and don't come home before eleven."

"You're telling me *not* to come home until a certain time. Like a reverse curfew?"

"Yep," he says, crossing his arms over his chest.

Brody starts to whimper from the living room instantly grabbing Amy's attention.

"Maybe I should—"

"Nope," Gareth and I say in unison, Gareth gently pushing his daughter out of the apartment at the same time as I grab her hand and pull her toward me.

"Have fun, do everything I would do and don't call me, I'll call you," he says and I don't miss the look of panic that crosses Amy's face.

"Really, guys. I'll just be a—" she stops mid sentence when her dad slams the door shut in her face. *That man's got balls the size of fucking Texas. I think I have a dude crush.*

She spins to face me. "Did he just do that? Oh my God, he really just did that."

"Sweetness," I say, giving her fingers a reassuring squeeze. "You know that Brody is totally fine. Your father would never let anything happen to him."

"Yeah, but—"

"We have reservations."

"But Dad doesn't know that."

"Actually he does."

"What?"

"Who do you think arranged for him to take care of Brodz?"

She falters and I take the opportunity to pull her down the corridor toward the elevator.

She directs her now narrowed eyes to mine.

"Fuck you're cute when you're wound up." She puts her

free hand on her hip, stopping me in my tracks, but not before I reach my arm out to push the call button.

"I'm not wound up. I'm half-pissed, half-impressed," she says, her expression one of adorable confusion.

Unable to resist any longer, I step forward and brush my lips against her temple, resisting every urge in me to kiss her. But I want the first time to be the best first kiss in the history of first kisses. One that brands her, burns into her soul and ruins her for all future kisses from anyone but me.

Her breath hitches and I know she feels it—whatever *it* is—that's going on between us. With a smile, I move away and lead her into the now open elevator.

A fifteen-minute drive later, I'm parking the car, opening her door, and leading Amy through the front doors of the restaurant, we're met by the wide smile of my friend Enrico, the owner and a former client of mine.

"Thomas," he says, placing his hand in my outstretched one and shaking it vigorously. He then turns his attention to Amy, his eyes moving back to mine and shining with approval.

"You, my man, are a very lucky man. She's beautiful." He steps forward, pulling Amy out of my reach and hugging her—a little too enthusiastically for my liking—eliciting a giggle from her mouth.

"Hi," she squeaks.

"Feel free to give my date back, Ricky," I muse.

"I don't think I want to," he shoots back, letting her go.

"Don't make me hurt you, old man."

"Why don't we let the lovely lady decide who the better man is?" he replies.

I chuckle when Amy moves back and takes my hand,

tangling her fingers back in mine and gratifyingly shifts to my side.

Enrico grabs his chest in mock hurt. "You wound me, *chiquita.*"

"The best man always wins," I say with a smirk.

"The good ones always do," he says back. "Now let me take you to your table."

"Is everything ready?" I ask quietly.

"As requested."

"What are you two whispering about?" Amy asks, quirking a brow.

"You'll see, sweetness," I say, dipping my head to kiss her forehead, the smell of her strawberry shampoo assaulting me in the best possible way.

She turns her now narrowed eyes on me. "Thomas, you've already done enough."

"Never," I say, squeezing her hand gently and leading her through the restaurant, up two flights of stairs behind Enrico.

When we reach a back door near the back of the restaurant, he turns to me, reaching up to clasp my shoulder.

"Enjoy, *mi hijo.*"

"Thank you," Amy calls out to his retreating back, giving a little squeak when I open the door and pull her inside, shutting it behind us. We both come to a jarring halt when we take in the sight before us.

I'd asked Enrico to make it special, my only specific requests being that a huge bouquet of flowers be left on the table for Amy when we arrived and that all of the food be plated so that we're not interrupted.

I didn't expect the room to be lit by a swath of candles lining the walls, the floor to ceiling windows showing off the shining lights of the city, and the most romantic table setting imaginable. Definitely over and above what I could ever have come up with. I make a note to leave Enrico an even bigger tip than usual when I pay the check.

Looking down at Amy, I know all of the work I put into this night was worth it. She meets my eyes, hers wet with unshed tears but I love that she doesn't hide her reaction.

"Thomas," she breathes in awe as her fingers squeeze mine.

I cup her jaw as my gaze roams her beautiful face and knowing the time is right, I lift her chin with my thumb and dip my mouth to brush against hers, not looking away out of fear of missing a single second of this moment.

Her lips part and her hand glides up my arm and around the back of my neck, holding me to her as I take that very first taste of her mouth, languidly stroking my tongue against hers and groaning into the kiss. I let go of her fingers but only to wrap my forearm around her back as her body melts into mine.

We stand there breathing each other in, and as corny as it sounds, if there was ever a moment where I wanted time to stand still and for the rest of the world to fade away, it's right now.

I ease back, loving the way she crinkles her nose and sighs when I rest my forehead against hers.

"I tried so fucking hard to wait 'til the end of the night but I couldn't hold back anymore."

"You don't ever have to hold back with me. I'm right where I want to be. Well, I was a few seconds ago anyway," she replies, her lips curling into a wry smile.

I grin. I can't fucking help it. I don't think I've ever been as happy as I am right now.

There's something to be said for taking one's time when they see something—or someone—they want.

With that in mind, I take a step back—more out of necessity than anything else—taking her hand in mine again and lead her to the table, pulling a chair out and pushing her in again once she takes a seat.

"The flowers are beautiful and the food smells amazing," she says when I take my seat opposite her.

"Only the best for you, sweetness." I lift the champagne out of the ice bucket and pour two glasses for us, handing one to her before grabbing my own.

I raise my hand, holding the flute in the air between us as she mimics the move.

"To friends, parents, and restaurant owners all stepping up to make me look good," I toast.

She giggles and gently clinks her glass with mine. "And to the sneaky man that asked them to do it, all for me." I chuckle and take a sip.

"You do realize you've set yourself up to fail now," she says, placing the drink back on the table.

"Oh really?" I sit back in my chair and take her in. "And why's that?"

"Because there's no way you're going to be able to top this night. I feel like a princess."

I reach over and grab her hand, brushing my lips over her knuckles. "Better get used to it then because I'm just getting started."

The food is delicious, the conversation between us seamless, but I know there's an elephant in the room that needs to be addressed. I mean, if I was her and I knew about it, I'd be dying to know the reasons why. How does one say 'Oh, by the way, the first time we have sex I'm likely to blow in a minute flat because I've been hard up for you for months and haven't had sex in over a year'?

It's not often a thirty-five-year-old man who lives hard, plays harder, and takes life one day at a time goes from sex on tap to nothing on the flip of a dime, or in my case the positive result of an STD test.

"Can I ask you a question?" she says.

"Of course but I'll tell you now, yes it's really nine inches, no I'm not joining the seminary and yes, no, maybe, and sixty-nine."

"Sixty-nine?"

"Everyone knows that the answer is always sixty-nine."

She bites her lip, taking a deep breath and slowly exhaling, drawing my attention to them. It just reminds me how much I want to kiss her again. How much I really want to do more than kiss her.

"So, nine inches?" she asks with a growing smile, her eyes dancing with amusement. This time I can't hold back my laughter.

"That's for me to know and you to find out," I tease. "Your question?"

Her eyes drop to the table and she tries to ease her fingers out of mine. I tighten my grip slightly and she stops, but she still doesn't say anything.

I give her time, waiting for her to talk because whatever she wants to know, I'll tell her. I want to move forward with her with nothing between us, no secrets, no lies, and no bullshit.

"Why have you . . ." she pauses and seems to steel herself before continuing, her eyes lifting to meet mine head on.

"Okay, so let's just get this out there. The girls talk, so you know that I know about—"

"Me not having sex in fifteen months?" Her eyes widen. She obviously didn't think it had been that long.

"Amz . . ." I say softly. "You can ask me anything. I'm an open book for you, I want you to know about me and I want you to want to know. Okay?"

She nods and I continue. "Up until last year, I was rather liberal in my appreciation of the female species."

Amy snorts then covers her mouth as she giggles.

"Yeah, okay. Massive understatement there."

"Maybe . . ." she says coyly, tilting her head to the side and looking fucking cute doing it.

"Then I had a situation and I decided that at thirty-four years of age, it was high time I stopped trying to stretch out my irresponsible twenties."

When I answer it's like her entire body relaxes. Her shoulders drop and she looks down to our joined hands, a blush creeping up her cheeks.

"Amz, I don't have a problem with you asking. Hell, I'm glad you asked. It's not exactly a great ice breaker now, is it?" She giggles and turns her hand over so we're palm to palm.

"No. But I want there to be nothing between us. I mean, you have already seen my lady bits so . . ."

"So you wanna see if I'm telling the truth about the nine inches?" I tease, moving my hand to my belt and going to stand up.

Her eyes grow wide and she spits out a laugh. "No! I meant it just seems like something we should probably get out of the way. I figured it was because of the . . . thing . . ."

I try hard to hold back my grin but when she's being cute as hell, it's near impossible not to smile.

"The thing? You mean cla-myd-ee-a aka the situation," I say with a grin. "It definitely wasn't fun at the time and it's not something I'm proud of but it gave me the kick up the ass I needed to sort myself out."

Her lips curl up and she tilts her head to the side. "You sure it wasn't the drink being thrown at you by the lovely lady in my bar?"

I throw my head back and bark out a laugh. "It could be. That definitely made an already bad day worse. Michelle is a special kind of human being."

"It was entertaining at the time, for me anyway."

"Funnily enough, that's not what I remember about that night," I reply, loving how relaxed she is and how she doesn't hold back with me.

"What do you mean?"

"You didn't judge me, you didn't give me shit—well, no more than a smart-ass bartender would anyway." She tilts her head, shrugging her shoulders apologetically. "You were just there for me."

A comfortable silence falls between us, my eyes dropping to her lips as she takes another sip of champagne.

"So was there a goal in deciding to not have sex?"

And that right there is one of the things that drew me to Amy. She doesn't shy away from anything with me anymore. A stark comparison to how she was with me before Brody's birth, before she fell asleep in my arms, and before Cade reaffirmed what I knew already, that I had anything but platonic feelings for her.

"Yeah, to give myself time and clarity to find exactly what I've been looking for."

She slants her head, her eyes studying me. "And what was that?"

"You."

Pulling up to the curb outside her building, I turn the car off and reach for the door handle, stopping when Amy places her hand on my arm.

"Thank you."

"Spending time with you tonight was thanks enough, sweetness."

Her eyes go soft in the second it takes me to say my pet name for her.

"I like you calling me that."

"I know," I reply with a grin. "But that's not what you're thanking me for, is it?"

"No," she says, biting her lip. She hesitates briefly but fuck it feels good when she reaches over the center console and places her hand over mine. "Thank you for tonight. For the dress, for the pampering, for everything."

I want to kiss her again. I *need* to kiss her again.

My eyes drop to her lips—which doesn't exactly help matters—and I imagine exactly how she'd taste and how much I want to hear her moan into my mouth.

Shit. Inappropriate boner in a semi-public place. Think of bad things. Totally non-sexy things. Definitely not her dusty pink lipstick and how I wouldn't give a fuck if I ended up wearing it all over my face if it meant I got to kiss the hell out of her right now.

Cold showers. Icy cold showers. I contemplate how cold Lake Michigan would be right now and whether jumping in fully clothed would do anything for my current predicament.

"Thomas?" she asks and meeting her eyes I see everything I want in that one look.

Swallowing hard, I turn my hand over to lace my fingers with hers. "I want to spoil you."

"But you don't—" I gently squeeze her fingers, cutting her off.

"I want you to know just how much I want to give this a shot. You've known part of me for a few years now, you've known more of me the past six weeks and I want to show you all of me from now on."

Her eyes move over my face, likes she's committing me—or this moment—to memory. She moves closer and lifts her hands to my face, pulling my mouth down to hers, taking control of the kiss and putting all thoughts of anything un-boner related out of my mind.

All I can think of is her. All I *want* to think about is her.

"One last thing," she says, giving me one last taste of her lips before leaning back in her seat, her perfect well-kissed mouth morphing into a satisfied smile.

"What's that?" I ask gruffly.

"With everything you've done tonight, you've totally nailed this first date thing."

"Glad to hear it."

She leans forward and beckons me in close with a crooked finger. "I'm really looking forward to seeing what else you can nail."

11

Amy

A week after our dinner date and I'm feeling out of sorts.

Not in a bad way, or a weird way, but a good way.

I'm *missing* Thomas. Unfortunately, he had to take a rain check on Takeout Thursday last night because of a business dinner he couldn't get out of. Not that I'd ever expect him to change a dinner just for me, and it did feel nice him intimating that he tried to reschedule, but I've become used to our regular Thursday night in.

In what I'm sure is a fact-finding mission—read: interrogation—Mia, Abi, Zoe, and Dani are currently residing in my living room for Friday night drinks. The excuse I was given was that the guys had moved their poker night forward and they were simply relocating their normal get-together to my place, but I know it's more than that.

"So . . . how's Thomas?" Abi asks, a knowing grin playing at her lips.

I narrow my eyes at my friend, shaking my head in the

process. "You *must* know considering Thomas is best friends with your husband."

She feigns shock, putting a hand over her heart. "And you think Cade would tell *me* about it?"

"If he didn't, then you probably tortured the information out of him," Mia says.

"You know me well," Abi replies. "But I want to hear Amy's version of events first before giving my commentary."

"There's a commentary?" Dani asks, quirking a brow.

"More like an opinion piece, a perspective from an outside observer," Abi replies.

Dani snickers. "You sound like me when you switch to intellectual speak."

"Oh, like you don't know, *Little Grasshopper,*" Abi says, using Zach's pet name for Dani. "I sat back and watched you and Zach go at it for months."

"You watched them? Like literally? Or are we talking metaphorically?" Zoe says, entering the conversation. "This conversation has definitely taken an unexpected turn."

I try hard not to giggle but the moment Mia gives up the ghost and bursts out laughing, I lose the fight. Soon enough, we're struggling to breathe, a situation that only gets worse when Dani snorts loudly sounding like a pig in heat. Or what I imagine a pig in heat might sound like.

"I don't mean literally. Not that a little visual stimulation is a bad thing. Just not one of my best friends," Abi continues once we all finally recover. She turns her attention to me, "But don't you dare try and change the subject, Amz. Spill or else I won't tell you what Thomas said."

I tilt my head and smirk. "Ever think that maybe I *know*

what Thomas thought of our date and that I don't *need* you to tell me?"

"Nope," she retorts back matter-of-factly. "Because you forget I know you. You *forget* that we *all* know you."

"We do?" Zoe says around a mouthful of corn chips. Mia just glares at her oldest sister, her eyes wide with surprise.

"Are you sure we're related?" she asks. Zoe just shrugs and again, we start giggling. This is what happens when they're one glass of wine in with husbands to drive them home at the end of the night. *Sober* husbands who enjoy the after-effects of their wives enjoying one too many drinks.

"Considering you two look more like twins than anyone else I know, yeah, I think we're all pretty sure you're related," Dani says.

"You do know that if you want to know about my date with Thomas, you kinda need to give me a chance to talk, right?"

"Oh, is *that* what has to happen to get you to spill? I thought I was going to ply you with alcohol," Abi states.

"No need," I say, lifting up my glass of cranberry juice in her direction before taking a sip. "You probably all already know that Thomas organized Mia to take me dress shopping." I look over to my best friend and wink at her, having already called her last Sunday to both ream her out for tricking me—half-heartedly of course—and thank her profusely for the part she played in getting me ready for the date.

"Well, Thomas also arranged my dad to babysit and for an old client of his to reserve a private dining room at this amazing Spanish restaurant in Humboldt Park."

"Jeez, that man went all out," Zoe murmurs, eyes riveted on me.

"And . . ." Dani presses, leaning forward in her chair.

"*And,* we talked, we had amazing food, he even had flowers waiting for me when we arrived."

"I think the boys need to take lessons," Mia muses, looking around the group. "Maybe Thomas can run a master-class, *How to score brownie points and guarantee porn-style head 101.*

"So . . . *Did* Thomas score brownie points?" Abi asks, a huge grin plastered on her face. I know she's loving this. She told me last year before 'STD-gate' and 'oops-I-got-knocked-up-gate' that she thought Thomas and I would be perfect for each other. In her words, 'then my best friend and Cade's best friend would be bumping uglies too.' Yes, my darling Abs has a special way with words. It's one of the things I love about her.

"Okay, enough with the buildup. Just tell us if you kissed —" Dani says.

"Or more than kissed, the more details the better," Mia adds.

My face heats up and I'm suddenly feeling uncharacteristically shy. I mean, these are my girls, the ones who helped me with cracked nipples and *everything* pregnancy related. I know I can tell them anything. And it's not like I put out on the first date.

Not that it felt like a first date. More like the tenth.

"Exactly," Abi says with a laugh.

"What?" I ask, looking up to find them all looking at me with amusement and I realize I just spoke all of my thoughts out loud.

"We *did* help you with everything baby and pregnancy related. They did anyway," she swings her arm over toward Mia and Zoe, the only other mothers in the group. "But yes, you can tell us anything and you better spill or I'll come over there and sit on you until you do."

I stare at her and she matches me, except she adds a raised eyebrow for good measure.

"Oh, all right. No, I didn't put out. Yes, we kissed. Twice. Maybe more than twice. The second and third could be counted as one . . . or maybe two . . . yes, definitely two."

"You know you're babbling, right?" says a now beaming Dani.

"Can I just say how much I love this? We needed some excitement since Abi and Cade are all 'happily married' now," Mia adds with air quotes.

Abi gasps and narrows her eyes at Mia. "Take that back. We're still interesting. I mean, Thomas walked in on us on the dining—"

"La la la," Dani says, putting her fingers in her ears. "I *really* don't need to know that."

Abi snorts, pointing her finger at Dani. "Like you can talk. Remember the morning of the wedding when I walked in on you and Zach fu—"

Moving quicker than I ever thought possible, Dani dives sideways, covering Abi's mouth with her hand. "*Anyway* . . . back to Amy . . ."

I can't help but laugh because for all Dani's protests, we all know there's a secret dirty girl beneath the geek exterior. A conversation last year about anal confirmed that and then some.

"So you kissed, and talked, and ate, and kissed again—*twice*—so what's next?"

I shrug. "I'm not sure. He couldn't come over last night for our weekly takeout and movie night—"

"There's a regular takeout and movie night?" Zoe asks, tilting her head to study me. "And how long has *that* been going on?"

"A few weeks, maybe a month?"

"You're right then. It wasn't really a first date. Well, it was and it wasn't. Therefore there's nothing wrong with a bit of slap and tickle between courses."

"The conversation didn't exactly lend itself to *anything* between courses."

"Oh?" she says. "Uncomfortable?"

"Not really, more serious. No, not serious, important maybe?"

"Maybe?" Abi asks. "How can something be not serious but important?"

"I asked him about not having sex for the past year."

"Now *this* I need to hear," Mia says. "I always wondered how a guy like Thomas can go from one hundred to zero in the blink of an eye. I mean, who *hasn't* had an STD before?" Three sets of wide eyes snap in her direction.

"Say what now?" Zoe splutters. "You've had an STD? When? How? And again, *when?*"

Mia waves us all off. "It was nothing. Just a case of crabs between friends. Two treatments ten days apart and I was good to go again."

The room goes deathly quiet. The only sound is the low hum of the television in the background and a buzz from Brody's baby monitor.

"What? It's nothing."

"You're right, it's nothing *now.* Who did you get it from? *How* did you get it? And *why* are we only finding out about this now?" Zoe says, repeating her unanswered questions.

"Enough about Mia, I want to hear about Amy kissing Thomas," Dani says, trying to steer the conversation back to me.

"You know we're going to talk about this later," Zoe says under her breath but Mia just rolls her eyes and moves her attention my way.

"I wanna know if there's going to be more kissing . . ."

"And *more* than kissing . . ."

"Yes, definitely that," Mia says. "Please tell us there's going to be more than kissing?"

I bite my lip and take a deep breath, deciding that there's no time like the present to ask them about the thing that's really bothering me.

"I want there to be more than kissing. A *lot* more. But it's been so long I wouldn't even know how to let him know I want it or that I'm ready to go there," I say quietly.

"Are you ready?" Zoe asks softly. "Because I remember being terrified the first time after Nate."

I meet her eyes. "I'm scared. But I think I'm ready, or at least willing to try," I reply with a small grin.

"Get naked in front of him," Mia says matter-of-factly like she's telling me the most obvious thing in the world.

"No, that's *too* obvious, especially for a first time," Abi says, standing up from the couch. She looks around the group. "Anyone for a top off?" When we all shake our heads, she walks out of the room and into the kitchen.

"Okaaaaay, so *don't* get naked?" I say slowly, my heart thudding against the side of my chest.

"Dress hot, act hot, *be* hot. He won't be able to resist," Zoe says.

"That doesn't tell him she wants him to jump her bones,"

Mia says. "Men are simple creatures. And if Thomas is trying to take this slow and be the respectful boyfriend candidate, he might miss something like that. I think you need to be more direct. Nothing tells a man you're horny and ready to get yourself some more than touching his dick."

This time I do spit out my drink, coughing and spluttering and making a big ol' mess on the floor.

"Anyway, I'm not sure jumping is what he'd be doing. More like nailing her into the mattress with his over-eager hammer," Mia murmurs with a giggle. Meems, always blunt and to the point. She's probably not wrong though.

"It's been how long for him?" Zoe asks.

"At least a year," Abi calls out from the kitchen.

"Then you'll definitely need to get the first time out of the way to get to the *second* time. That will be the rock-your-world sex. First time out of the gate for both of you after a long dry spell is going to be hard and fast," Mia says.

Abi walks back into the room nodding. "Definitely fast."

"Unless he pre-games. Then he'd be fine," Dani says.

"Um, *hello.* So you're telling me to get naked and jump him and also expect the first time to be a wham bam 'blow his load quicker than a virgin on prom night.' Did I get that right?"

They don't say anything, they just look at me and grin.

"Can't wait till the 'after-sex' debrief. This is fun," Dani says, bouncing in her seat.

Definitely looking forward to that one now.

After the girls have all been collected by their grinning and—in Mia's case, positively beaming—husbands, I put on a

Nicholas Sparks movie with Channing Tatum in it, and snuggle down under a blanket on the couch.

Picking up my phone and checking that it's not too late, I send Thomas a message.

Amy: How was poker night?

Thomas: Not so good. Sean was on a streak and cleaned us all out.

Amy: Oh well, you can't win them all.

Thomas: I still think I'm coming out on top. Well I will be if you let me take you and Brody out tomorrow . . .

Amy: We'd love to. What do you have planned?

Thomas: It's a surprise.

Amy: Something to know about me, I'm not a fan of surprises. That's why I found out Brody's sex as soon as I could,

Thomas: This will be a good surprise, I promise. You liked my first surprise date, didn't you?

Amy: You know I did.

Thomas: So have some faith in me.

Amy: I do.

Thomas: Good. How was your night?

Amy: Good. I got grilled about our date by the girls.

Thomas: Abi was there when Cade did the same to me last weekend.

Amy: I know that too. She seems to be a fan of Team Thamz.

Thomas: Team Thamz?

Amy: That's our couple name apparently. All the celebrities have them.

Thomas: And we're celebrities now?

Amy: Definitely a hot topic apparently.

Thomas: It does have a nice ring to it. How's the boy today?

Okay, *whoosh.* Maybe even a mega whoosh. I love how much he cares about my son.

Amy: He's good. Went down straight away after being fawned over by a room full of women.

Thomas: I think any man would do the same thing.

Amy: Go down?

He doesn't reply straight away and I imagine him sitting at home, maybe in front of his television, biting his tongue—figuratively and literally—trying not to reply back with the first thing that comes to mind. Knowing Thomas, it would be undoubtedly dirty.

Part of me is hoping he'll reply back with whatever his first thought is.

Thomas: Are you trying to torture me now? Been taking lessons from Abi?

Amy: Maybe I taught her everything she knows . . .

Thomas: Now that is an intriguing thought and one I look forward to investigating further.

Amy: You think I'm going to let you get off that easy?

Again I wait a few minutes before my phone vibrates with his reply.

Thomas: You're killing me here, sweetness.

Amy: That's funny. I thought I was only getting started.

Thomas: Does lunch time tomorrow sound good?

I let him get away with the change in subject. He may be a reformed playboy but I also know that he's holding back where I'm concerned, not because he's not interested—definitely not if the end of date kiss is anything to go by—but out of respect for me and the us that we're building.

Amy: Perfect. I can feed Brody before we go and he can sleep in the baby carrier.

Thomas: Sweet dreams, Amy. Try not to think of me *too* much ;)

Amy: I wasn't going to be thinking of you, but now I don't think I'll be able to do anything but. If you're woken up by messages at Brody's 3 a.m. feeding, you'll only have yourself to blame.

Thomas: You can message me day or night. *Especially* if you're thinking of me. I definitely want to know about that. See you tomorrow.

12

Amy

"Hi," I say, opening the front door when he arrives the next afternoon.

Without saying a word, Thomas steps forward, wraps a hand around my neck and pulls me toward him before he crushes his mouth against mine.

It takes everything in me not to moan into his mouth despite everything in my body screaming out to do so. But as quick as it starts, he forces himself back, his blue eyes threatening to scorch me alive right there in my doorway.

"Hi," he says hoarsely. "You look amazing." He doesn't move away but his eyes take in everything they can see. There was one piece of advice I took out of the girl's chat yesterday; the 'look hot, be hot' recommendation.

"If that's how you greet me now, we should've started dating months ago," I muse, instinctively lifting my hand to my mouth, tracing my tingling bottom lip with my thumb.

He shakes his head and grins down at me. "You gonna let me in, sweetness?"

Is it me, or is there some double entendre at play here. I thought I had let him in? And if I hadn't, there's no doubt I have since last week.

" . . . or is our second date going to be on your landing?" he continues.

Right. Overthinking again, Amz. Good one. "Oh, I suppose," I say in mock annoyance, stepping aside.

"Much obliged." His lips twitch and he gives my hip a gentle squeeze as he walks past.

"Let me just get Brody's bag and we can go if you like. He's been a bit out of sorts today, just grizzly and unsettled. I'm sure he's fine though. He'll have a nap and wake up happy again," I jabber on, walking toward Brody's room.

"I'll get the baby," Thomas says, stepping around me and bending down, picking up my son in what seems like such a normal everyday occurrence. Like we do this every day. Like we're a couple getting our son ready to go out. And again, I'm left wishing that my asshole radar wasn't so wonky when my vagina chose Brody's father. Mainly because the more time I spend with Thomas, in the new version of us that we're working on now, the *dating* version of us, the more I want everything normal with him.

The normal us that is Thomas, me and Brody. Going out. Doing family stuff. Together.

The three of us against the world.

My mind clears of everything except the feelings swirling inside of me. Feelings I never thought I'd get to act on—not that we have yet—but still, I certainly never envisioned I'd be dating Thomas, that I'd even be contemplating dating anyone following a hard pregnancy, that memorable birth, and with an eleven-week-old son who is the center of my world.

I look out the window and watch the world pass by, content for the first time in a long while and it's because of one man.

The only reason it has happened is because it's Thomas. The only reason I think I've allowed it to happen is because of Thomas.

"I think Mommy was just away with the fairies, Brodz. Do you think we should leave her to frolic with the butterflies or should we take her to our surprise destination?"

That snaps me out of my daze.

"You're going to kidnap my son right in front of me?" I ask, quirking a brow.

He looks down at Brody then back to me. "I think we'd both rather have you come too."

"Right. Let's go then." My tone is a little huffy, but it's all for show.

I turn around to grab my keys and purse from the dining room table. I feel Thomas come up close behind me, the heat of his body warming me from head to toe, making me tremble. A condition that only worsens when his breath fans across the bare skin of my neck.

"It wouldn't be the same without you. You make everything better just being there."

Thunk. That's the sound of my heart stopping dead in my chest. I swear to God if my son wasn't in his arms—hell, if he wasn't in the room—I'd spin around and jump Thomas right now.

"Good," I say, exhaling the breath that catches in my chest.

He presses his lips gently to that magic spot below my ear and reaches down, entwining his fingers with mine in the same way he did the other night. The move that never fails to give me a big ol' whoosh in all the right places.

Brody grizzles and starts pulling his legs up in Thomas's arms, almost fighting him.

"C'mon buddy, it's okay," Thomas says, lifting his hand to rub Brody's back. When Brody ramps up the crying, I decide I need to step in.

I drop the baby bag by the front door and hold my arms out to a now nervous looking Thomas.

"I don't know what's wrong. He might have gas or maybe he's coming down with something." I place the back of my hand on Brody's forehead, frowning at the heat I feel that wasn't there before. Realizing that my baby is sick and not just being fussy, a tsunami wave of guilt washes through me. I was about to drag him out on a date.

Mother of the freaking year here.

"I think he's got a fever," I say, moving across my apartment toward the living room "What do I do when he's got a fever?" I look to Thomas as if expecting him to have the answers. "He's not even three months old. I don't know what to do."

"It's fine, Amz. We'll stay in and watch him. If he gets worse, we'll take him to the ER."

I cradle Brody in my arms, feeling his nose rooting into my chest, his tell-tale sign that he wants to nurse. "I'm going to nurse him and maybe strip his clothes off. I need to take his temperature too."

And like an anchor in a storm, Thomas changes tact, taking control of the situation and as always, proves that he's more of an adult than anyone else I know.

"If you're okay for a few minutes, I just need to go get some things from my car and we can have our date here."

"I'm really sorry, Thomas."

He walks over and puts an arm around my shoulders to where I'm now nursing Brody, cocooning both of us in his arms. "Sweetness, I don't want you to ever apologize for being a good mom. Brody comes first. Hopefully, I'm somewhere in the top five and rising," he says with a wry grin. He leans in and brushes his lips against mine. "You finish feeding him. I'll call Cade and just check with him what we should be doing. I'll be back in a couple of minutes and we'll come up with a plan. Sound good?"

I nod and blink to fight back my stinging eyes.

"See you in a few minutes," I say to his back, watching him walk out just as I hear a burp, a gurgle, and then feel Brody spit up all down my front.

Totally not looking hot now, Amz.

Two hours and two calls to Cade later, when it appears that my spewing exorcist baby has worn himself out and I'm giving him one more feed in his room, Thomas takes the opportunity to jump in the shower to de-vomit himself.

When Brody finally gives up the fight for sleep while nestled into my chest, I put him down in his crib and quickly go to my room to get changed. This plan is good in theory, except for the sound of the bathroom door opening while I'm standing there in nothing but my bra and panties, caught with my shirt mid-removal. And since I wasn't expecting Thomas to actually *see* my underwear today, it's not exactly the sexiest set I own. In fact, point me toward any nursing bras that can be called 'desirable' and I might just call you a liar.

I instinctively jerk the rest of the top off with a shriek and come face to face with a towel-clad Thomas wearing *nothing* but a towel. His dark blond hair shoots off in every possible direction and his bare chest is covered in nothing but stray drops of water.

My mouth waters at the sight and not only that, I'm thirsty —ravenous—with the need to lick away every. Single. Drop.

"Ah, hi . . ." I stutter, clutching my tee to my chest and hoping the girls are covered.

His wide eyes turn warm . . . then hot . . . then scorching as he scans me head to toe and back up again.

Yes, the man may have seen my vagina already, but right now I feel more exposed than ever.

"Looking good there, sweetness," he says, his voice carrying a rasp that does delicious and almost embarrassing things to my body.

I'm too mesmerized by his hand and the towel and the way he's drying all of the drops of water from his chest, every swipe a damn shame.

"Amz?" he says, his gaze amused as he watches me and I'm snapped out of my carnal admiration, the reality of the situation seeping in.

"Um . . ." I whisper.

"Fuck you're adorable." No, I'm half naked in my bedroom with a half-naked Thomas and the sudden need for some alone time in order to thoroughly enjoy the sight in front of me is overwhelming.

"You *do* know this is my bedroom right?"

"Yup," he replies, the corner of his mouth turning up. "I kinda figured Brody was still holding you hostage, but I'm not complaining at the view I get instead."

I snort and shake my head, my grip on my tee slipping and before I realize, my lace covered girls announce their existence. Thomas's eyes drop as if drawn by a magnetic boob force field, his Adam's apple bobbing as he swallows hard but interestingly doesn't politely look away.

It's not like we're strictly platonic at this stage. We were supposed to have had our second date today, although when I think back to the amount of time Thomas and I have spent together, it's more like we've almost reached the four-month mark.

Heat courses through me and I don't miss the flash of heat in his eyes matching the wave of awareness sweeping through me. I clear my throat, biting my lip to stop myself from laughing, swooning, and melting into a puddle at his feet all at the same time.

He meets my gaze and I swear his cheeks are a little flushed and *not* from the shower. "I'll just go get changed in the other room."

Right. So he's removing himself from temptation. Interesting.

"Okay. I'll be out in a minute. I might just grab a shower myself while I've got the chance."

"Go for it. I'll listen out for Brodz." Hearing the half-naked man you're kind of dating say he'll help you with your son? *Mega whoosh.*

But instead of turning for the door and exiting as I expected, he closes the four steps between us and gently rests his hands on my waist, pulling me to him. My bare thighs meet the soft towel wrapped around his hips and the hard—freaking titanium hard—bulge against my stomach is unmistakable. *Maybe he wasn't just boasting about nine inches.*

"You okay?"

I nod. Biting my lip to stop anything utterly embarrassing or completely inappropriate from leaving my mouth.

"Can I ask you something? And I'm totally fine if you say no, or aren't ready yet." My breath catches in my throat. Ah shit. Surely he's not going to ask if we can have sex.

"Sure," I croak out, sounding totally unattractive.

His lips twitch. "Sweetness," he says softly and I feel his voice caress me from the top of my head to the tips of my toes. "I want to stay the night with you and help you out with Brodz if he gets sick again."

Well doesn't *that* cause a whoosh in all the right places.

"I can sleep on the couch. I totally understand if you're not ready to share a bed with me or if you're uncomfortable, but—"

I swallow, not wanting to sound like a frog on crack when I reply this time. "That would be good."

His eyes go warm and he beams down at me. "Thank you, for letting me have this," he says before dipping his head and placing a gentle kiss on my forehead.

This? What's this? Staying the night? Peace of mind? *Me?*

I'm not far off being ready for a ride on the Thomas train but I totally won't be able to relax if I know my nearly three-month-old son is sick in the room beside us.

"I really need to get in the shower . . ."

He blinks, almost like he expected me to say something else, but recovers just as quickly.

"Sure, sorry," he says, stepping out of my bubble.

"I'll just go get dressed while you're cleaning up."

"Cool. Yeah, thanks. Um, I'll be back soon," I rush out, struggling to keep my breathing even as I walk around him to the dresser, grab a tee and some pajama shorts, and move into the bathroom, shutting the door a bit too quickly to not be completely obvious.

I manage to get through my shower without passing out but the minute I hop out and get dressed, I grab hold of the vanity and stare at myself in the mirror as my brain hits hyper drive.

My legs are shaking, my heart pounding and my body is strung tight.

I'm no virgin, and Thomas is no choirboy going by the strength of his game and his former friend, chlamydia—but there's been so much build up to this that I'm a nervous wreck.

I used to be unapologetic about my body, my experience, my wants and needs. It's been so long since I've even thought about sex, that now that I'm here, it's like I'm v-card holder all over again.

I know that the penis goes into the vagina. I know what feels good, what feels great, and what feels fucking phenomenal. I know positions, actions, what hand goes where and that if you hook one leg he can go nice and deep.

But even knowing all of that, I can't stop my mind from going into freak out mode.

What if it hurts? What if it's like throwing a sausage down a state highway? What if something goes wrong, the condom breaks, the universe conspires against me and I get knocked up again? What if I'm just a convenient pussy with a pulse? What if he only lasts for three pumps and a dump?

Then I think back to the advice the girls gave me about just letting him know when I'm ready. Maybe not so much of Mia's 'touch his dick' suggestion though. I might not take that direct of an approach.

Shit, what if I do 'make a move' and he rebuffs the offer. That would be more than embarrassing.

I'm trying to breathe through my self-imposed panic attack when a gentle knock comes from the closed door behind me. I go completely still, so much so I even stop breathing, a small part of me hoping he'll suddenly forget that I'm hiding out in the bathroom.

"I can hear your brain working from out here, Amz."

"I—" I squeak, clearing my throat, "I'm just getting ready for bed."

"Amz, you forget how well I know you."

"I'll be out in a minute," I reply, thankfully sounding more self-assured than I'm feeling.

The door handle rattles, the only warning I get before the stubborn, beautiful, fantasy man who's turned me inside out, upside down, and back up again, is standing in the mirror behind me, his eyes soft as they meet mine.

"Stop thinking," he says, his hands moving to frame my hips as he steps forward and brings his chest flush against my back. "Stop worrying." He drops his mouth to my bare shoulder and grazes his lips along my skin and up to that magic money spot just below my ear. "We're just going to sleep, nothing more. I just want to get into bed and literally sleep with you in my arms. Then, if Brody wakes up in the night, I'm here to help you out. It'll give me peace of mind. Can you give me that, sweetness?"

Now I'm panicking for a different reason. Not because I'm going to be sharing a bed with Thomas. No, it's more about the fact that he *only* wants to sleep. There's no playful banter, no hooded eyes and dark heated looks in the mirror shining back at me. He *literally* wants to sleep.

How can a hot-blooded man like him *not* want to do anything?

I mean, I'm hot. I'm sexy. I'm ready to jump back on the

horse but now I'm the pent up one and *he* is the one with self-control.

Is this some parallel universe or something?

My internal freak out is interrupted the moment Thomas links his fingers with mine and pulls me out of the bathroom, leading me toward the bed where he sits and pulls me down, forcing me to straddle his legs and put my knees on the mattress on either side of him.

He looks up at me, his expression one of soft amusement. "You're adorable when you pout."

"I'm not p—" His hands circle my waist making my breath catch.

"Don't ever think I don't want you, Amz. I've waited a long time for you but I want to do this right, and I want to make sure we're both ready for what it will mean when I'm inside you for the first time."

"I—" His fingers tense and I stop talking, loving the way his eyes crinkle when I do. I've noticed that they always do that when I do something he likes.

"Maybe you're ready, maybe you're not, but it needs to be perfect. I *want* it to be perfect because the one thing you might not know about my vow of abstinence is that I promised myself that the next woman I took to bed would also be the last one." He lets that hang between us and I'm glad that he does because it kinda says it all.

I'm speechless. Absolutely fucking speechless. What does a woman say to that? I mean, my dating experience pre Brody was pretty epic but I never met someone like Thomas, someone so sure of themselves and what they want, *who* they want.

And he's telling me that the last woman he'll ever sleep with is me.

Me.

Well, heck. He can take all the time in the world then. I've got a vibrator, I can take care of business until he's ready to take care of it for me.

"Yeah," I whisper, unable to look away from this beautiful man laying it all out there for me.

"Good," he replies back, just as quietly. He lifts his hands to my face and pulls my mouth down to his for a soul-feeding, heart exploding kiss that cements his words—his vow—in my mind, my body, and everywhere else that may have needed reminding.

Pulling back a touch, he brushes his lips against mine one more time then stays there to whisper, "I've locked up the house and turned everything off, so how about we get into bed and catch some sleep before the lord and master of the manor wakes up again."

Belly flip, pussy quiver and heart thud, all at once.

There's no way I'll ever forget this moment or the life-changing whoosh I just experienced. Not on your life.

Not that I'd ever want to anyway.

"Just saying," I add once we're both settled underneath the covers, Thomas spooning me from behind. "I can totally take care of myself until you're ready. Just thought you should know."

The responding groan I hear from behind me makes up for all my neurotic ramblings earlier.

"Not helping, sweetness," he says as the evidence of what I'm not helping makes its presence clear against my ass.

"Don't worry, I won't need your help. I've got everything I

need in a perfect seven and a half inch pocket rocket in my drawer."

"Keep it up and I'll test out the theory, and sweetness?" he says, nipping my ear, his voice a low growl. "When I say test, I mean *thoroughly*."

"Is that a threat or a promise?"

"It's a goddamn guarantee."

13

Thomas

I never would wish Brody to be sick again, but I can't say I'm not grateful for it since it served as the catalyst for me staying the night in Amy's bed for the first time, in the same house as the two people who have come to be among the most important in my life.

Waking up with Amy in my arms for the first time, her body plastered to my side from chest to thigh is something I'll never forget and in the month since then, has been repeated on a regular basis.

And although I'm over there a *lot* now, I still haven't pushed her for anything more than making out on her couch, or her bed.

I don't want to push her and I don't want to make any mistakes when it comes to the physical side of our relationship because I meant what I said to her and Cade all those months ago: The next woman I have sex with will be the last. I know I want it to be Amy, but I think it's now come to the point where

I've built it up so much in my head about how our first time together will be, I'm not willing to take a chance of anything going wrong when we do get down to it.

However, it's safe to say that I've been taking a hell of a lot of long showers in recent times and if I thought I jerked off a lot in the past year without having sex, knowing I'm close to having it and not wanting to blow it, my hand and my dick have had an intense monogamous relationship. Multiple times a day too.

Of all the things I've missed about sex, it's the taste of a woman. It's the smell of her, that tell-tale scent igniting my senses, making my mouth water in anticipation. Then that first lash of my tongue against her skin. A slow languid brush; an introduction, a tease, and a promise of all the good things destined to come.

When I get Amy naked and ready for me, I want all the time in the world to study, taste, touch, lick, sip and suck every damn inch of her before giving her everything that is me.

I've come to terms with my growing feelings for Amy as well as the strong bond forming between her son and me.

That's not to say Amy and I haven't progressed a little bit at least. There have been a few hot and heavy make out sessions on her couch that drew close to crossing the line but as if he knew what was happening, Brody always seems to have a knack of knowing the exact wrong time to wake up.

Lucky he's cute and I love the little guy as if he was my own.

Today is going to be the turning point. The last thing on my list to tick off before I'm absolutely sure that I can trust myself to escalate festivities from solo efforts to mind-blowing sex.

Once I've introduced Amy and Brody to my mom and dad, then I'll step up the planning for my first time with Amy. Just like the first date, I want everything to be perfect. I've already set some things in motion, the rest is just waiting for the right moment.

"Stop fidgeting, it's going to be fine," I say, reaching over the center console to grab Amy's hand.

She turns my way, her gaze pinning me in place. "It's a rite of passage for a woman to be nervous the first time she meets the parents of the man she's . . . um . . ."

"Dating?"

"Yes, dating," she huffs. She turns her hand over to tangle her fingers in mine, giving them a gentle squeeze. "I haven't done the whole 'meet the parents' thing before. You're gonna have to cut me a little bit of slack in the freak out department."

"I have a whole new respect for what Daniel went through with Mac now," I mutter under my breath. Her grip tenses and I know she heard me.

"I know how prone Mac is to freak outs. I've heard all about them from Dani and Zoe, and even from Mac herself. All women have moments where they have so many thoughts going through their head it can take a few moments to process them all at once."

"Sweetness—"

"I know I'm a lot to take on and believe me when I say that I'm fully aware that I have baggage, but—"

Now it's my turn to flex my fingers. "You don't ever have to think of your son as baggage. He is just as important to me as you are, and that's a fuck of a lot and it grows more and more every day." Her breath catches but I power through it, knowing I can't do anything except drive and talk right now. Doesn't mean I can't think about all the ways I wish I could calm her nerves right now though. Many, many ways I've thought about in great detail over the past few weeks.

"I care about you too," she says softly, a sound that reverberates through my body straight down to my dick. "I'm just saying that I know this isn't your normal 'boy meets girl' situation and I . . ." she pauses for a moment, "I really want your parents to like me."

Thanking the Lord for all things holy, I have to slow down for a red light, giving me the chance to give her my full attention.

"Sweetness, my mother already loves you and she's never even met you."

"But how . . ." she stops and her eyes widen when the realization hits her.

"You've told her about me?"

"Yep, and Brody. A *lot.* I'm very close to my parents, I respect their opinions and I'm always turning to them for help and guidance. When I made the decision that I was going to act on my feelings for you, my mother was the first to warn me about everything that I had to be careful of. Mainly the fact that it wasn't just the two of us in this relationship; it will always be the three of us. You, me, and Brody."

"But—"

"*And,*" I say, stopping her with another squeeze, "and I love that about us. I knew that I wasn't just getting to know you and spending time with you, I was also spending time with Brody, letting him get to know me, and what I have with him and what we have may be separate, but they are also very much connected."

"Thomas . . ."

"And not once has it even entered my mind that Brody is *baggage,*" I finish.

"Um . . . the light's green," she says with a wry smile.

"Oh," I say, turning back to face the road just as another car honks their horn behind us.

Taking off, I move forward, taking a right into my parents' neighborhood.

"Suddenly I'm not feeling as nervous anymore."

"Good," I say gruffly.

She leans into my side so her mouth is right by my ear. "And if it were possible, I'd totally kiss you right now," she whispers huskily.

I tighten my grip on the steering wheel and keep my eyes to the front, knowing exactly what my head, body—and especially my hard-on—would like to do with that comment.

It hasn't been lost on me that Amy is ready to take the next step in our relationship, and I'm fully on board with that. I'm just . . . nervous. Totally unlike me. In business, I'm known to be ruthless. Direct and to the point, I don't fuck around when it comes to making decisions or taking action.

With sex before Amy, I was the same. If I saw a woman I was interested in, I'd go for it, knowing full well that she could shoot me down but happy to take that risk regardless.

I know sex with Amy is going to be more than physical. And for a man like me who has never seen sex as anything other than a physical act, this is a big thing. Huge. Monumental. Life changing.

Something that sex never has been with me.

Something that I know will alter our relationship and life between us as soon as I'm inside her.

I'll probably only last a minute though. I mean, it has been well over a year now and jerking off is all well and good, but nothing compares to the real thing.

My thoughts on the topic clear when I see my parents' mailbox and turning into their driveway causes the atmosphere in the car to grow thick again as Amy moves back to sit ramrod straight in her seat, her eyes glued to the two story home in front of us.

"Shit, shit, damn," Amy mutters, her breaths coming quicker now, all previous sexy murmurings in my ear all but forgotten.

"You're gonna be fine. I've also got a surprise for you."

"What?" she asks, her voice tight.

"Mom and Dad wanted to have a barbecue and I thought you'd be more comfortable if you had some familiar faces here so Abi and Cade are coming too."

"Oh thank God," she breathes, her shoulders slumping in relief. Her arm reaches around my shoulders and she moves closer, pulling me into a hug. Needing more, I slide my hand into her hair and pull her head back just enough so I can touch my lips to hers. Running my tongue along the seam of her mouth, she relaxes and lets me in, allowing me to deepen the kiss as my arm tightens around her chest, holding her to me.

A knock on the passenger window breaks the moment and we both turn our heads to come face to face with my grinning father.

"Oh my God," Amy whispers, and all relaxation is gone. I cup her face, bringing her attention back to me, brushing my lips against hers and leaving them there.

"Remember what I said, they already love you."

Her eyes search mine as if looking for any ounce of doubt, but there's none to be found.

"Okay," she whispers and my own body relaxes, letting go of tension I didn't realize I was holding.

"Let's go, I know Mom is dying to meet the woman who's put a smile on her son's face."

She stills and I brace for freak out number two, but instead she just smiles brightly at me.

"We better get inside then. Can't keep her waiting."

With a nod to Dad, I step out of the car just as he opens the passenger door and pulls her in for a hug. "Well, aren't you gorgeous. You caught yourself a good one here, son."

"I think so," I muse, leaning into the car to pull Brody's car seat out, careful not to wake him up since he drifted off about ten minutes into the drive.

"I'm Albie. Thomas has been telling us about you for months now," Dad tells Amy, leading her toward the front porch of the house with one arm around her shoulders.

"Oh really?" she asks, saying her first words since leaving the car but just hearing her sass make a welcome return has me breathing a sigh of relief.

"Dad, you wanna give me a chance here? I'm trying to impress her with my masculine charm and you're kind of undercutting that."

Amy looks over her shoulder at me and winks. "Don't worry, baby, I promise to never question your manliness in public."

"She's going to keep you on your toes, son. Just like your mother does with me," Dad says with a laugh just as he swings open their front door, coming face to face with my mom. "Speaking of my lovely wife. Amy, this is Edie."

"Hi Edie, it's a pleasure to meet you," Amy says, holding out her hand for Mom to shake. Mom being Mom looks down at the hand and shakes her head, tutting a few times before grabbing Amy's arm and jerking her in for another hug.

Jeez, the parentals are laying it on thick today. Two hugs in less than a few minutes. I'll have to keep Brody away from them for a little while. The poor guy will be lucky to spend a moment alone at this rate.

"Hi Mom, remember me? Your son?" I say, grinning when her eyes move over Amy's shoulder to me.

"Hmmm, give me a minute. I seem to remember having a son once. He was dashingly handsome and loved wearing Captain Planet underwear right up until he left for college."

"Nicely played, Mom," I say with a chuckle, moving through the front door and grabbing Amy's hand on the way through, before leading her into the family room.

"Captain Planet? I would've bet you were more of a Superman kind of guy," she murmurs for my ears only. I grin and shake my head, my eyes meeting hers, not missing the depth of promise I see there.

I put Brody's baby seat on the sofa, waiting until Amy takes a seat beside him before letting either of them go.

"Would you like a drink, dear?" Mom asks from the doorway. I turn around, opening my mouth saying, "I'll get something, Mom," just as Amy replies, "water or juice would be great, thank you, Mrs. Caldwell."

Amy and I look at each other and snicker before looking to my mother. I shrug and smirk at her. "I guess old habits die hard. That was for Amy, wasn't it?"

Mom laughs, "Yes, Thomas. I always serve guests before

family. You know that. But, since you offered, you can get Amy a water or juice and pour me a glass of white wine while I get to know your lovely date and her beautiful baby." She walks toward us and it's then the baby talk starts. "Oh look at him, he's such a beautiful boy," she says.

"Don't embarrass me, Mom. I swear if you pull out my baby photos I'll have to disinherit you or something."

"Isn't that something I should say to you?" Dad says, entering the fray.

"Hey, I went to business school, not law school. Just don't scare her off. I like her having me around." I shoot Amy a wink before leaving the room and hoping I haven't just thrown her to the wolves.

I needn't have worried. Over the next hour, Mom and Dad charmed Amy—and vice versa with her winning them over—so much so I wondered if I needed to even be there. That's how well they were all getting along. When Cade and Abi arrived, it was like I was the seventh wheel.

When Brody wakes up from his nap and I lift him out of his baby seat to give him to Amy, I don't miss Mom's blissful expression.

"I always missed the whole nursing thing. When we got Thomas he was already a young man and well past the need for bottles. Wouldn't change it for the world though."

Amy's eyes meet mine as she takes Brody from my arms, and I read her unspoken question there. I hadn't told her about being adopted. To be honest, it's not something that I hide but it's also not something I spread far and wide. Mainly because —as far as I'm concerned—my parents Albie and Edie are the only ones I've ever known and are therefore exactly that, my parents. They took me on at eight and have not once treated me like I was anything but their own blood.

It's probably why I managed to get through high school, college, and my adult life so far without even a speeding ticket to my name.

Well, that could also be because I was always careful enough never to get caught, but that's a story for another day.

"You were adopted?" she says quietly when I bring my lips to her temple.

"Yeah, sweetness. But to me, they're just my parents. Family isn't always blood," I say, dropping my forehead to hers before stepping back and taking a seat beside them. I reach down to the baby bag and rummage inside for a blanket before handing it to Amy and helping her cover herself up to feed Brody.

"I'm going to fire up the grill. The rest of the dinner guests should arrive soon so we might as well get ready. Thomas, would you like to come help?"

"Sure, Dad." I pin Mom with a playful glare. "You play nice now, Mom."

"Oh pffft," she says waving me away. "I'm not scary."

"Maybe I'm worried for your safety, not Amy's," I add with a grin.

Amy gasps and narrows her eyes at me. "I promise not to scare your mom away, Thomas," she says in a sing-song voice.

"Glad to hear it, sweetness. Now I better go save the grill from Dad. He's not exactly known for his culinary skills."

"And you are?" she says, quirking a brow. I look down to see Brody also staring up at me, still suckling. "You're the king of takeout."

"Only on Thursdays," I reply, hoping she remembers the last Takeout Thursday when food was the last thing on our mind. She blushes and I shoot her a wink before walking out of the room, holding out hope that Mom won't resort to embarrassing stories to 'win' Amy over.

14

Thomas

"Dinner was nice," Amy says, staring out the window as we head toward her place.

"It was. Didn't I tell you my parents would love you?"

"You did. I'm glad you were right."

"Me too," I add with a chuckle. The car goes quiet again, Brody having fallen asleep in my arms shortly after dinner had ended and remained out still.

"Can I ask you something?" Amy says, a few minutes later.

"Anything . . ."

"Why haven't you told me you were adopted?"

"I honestly don't know. I don't see them as my adoptive parents. To me, they've always been Mom and Dad. They're the two people who saw something in me where others didn't and gave me the home I always wanted and needed."

"Do you . . . actually, never mind."

I squeeze her knee gently. "You can ask me anything, Amz. I'll tell you anything you want to know."

Again, she falls quiet and I swear I can hear her brain ticking over.

"Do you feel close to Brody because you know what it's like not to have a biological parent?" I don't even have to think twice before answering.

"He doesn't need a father, he has you. But to answer your question, no." I take a slow calming breath, wondering why her thinking that pisses me off a little bit.

"I didn't mean—"

"I'm close to Brody because I helped bring him into the world and in getting to know you, I got to know him. You and him are a package deal but I can tell you right now that what I have with you two has *nothing*—not one thing—to do with me being adopted or not knowing my birth parents."

"Do you wish you had known them? Remembered your birth parents?" I think on that one. It's something I have thought about a lot over the years.

"Sean looked them up for me a while ago. My birth mother died of an overdose a few years after I was adopted, my birth father was never listed."

Thankfully, I've pulled into Amy's parking garage by the time I finish speaking, bring my car to a stop and turned the car off.

I don't get to say anything else because it's then that Amy leans over the center console and rubs her hand up my leg, dragging her fingers over my thigh then her palm over my groin. My grip on the steering wheel tightens as I try to remember all of the most unsexy sights I can imagine.

My mother. *No, not my mother, not right now.*

Petri dishes. Fourth quarter market results. Audit recommendations. *Anything.*

She runs her tongue up the side of my neck, her other arm wrapped around my shoulder as she sucks my earlobe between her lips. She's upped the ante and I'm so unprepared. I've been fighting my own battle, trying to resist the urge to forget all plans to make our first time together memorable and just taking her up on the many offered opportunities she's availed to me.

The first time I make love to Amy I want it to be done right . . . and slow . . . *very* slow. Not in the front seat in a parking garage.

"Let's get Brody upstairs and then we can talk," I rush out, failing to quell my aching need to take her here and now. This isn't how I wanted our first time to be. It has to be perfect.

"It's okay. Just forget it," she says sharply. Opening her door, she jumps out of the car, even grabbing Brody and his car seat before I can round the trunk.

Taking the baby seat from her hands, I carry Brody on one arm and entwine my fingers with Amy's, leading her toward the elevator and not letting go until we're all safely enclosed in her apartment.

She lifts Brody out of the seat and looks to me. "I'm just going to put him down and then I'll be back." Her voice is tight but she doesn't linger, turning on her heels and walking down the hall toward the bedrooms.

I may be a hapless male at times but I've spent enough time with Amy to know when something is up with her, and one of those times is now.

I'm almost certain Abi would know what's wrong but I'm not sure I'm prepared to text her with my figurative tail between my legs, asking for her help.

I've turned the TV on, opened a bottle of wine and poured

two glasses for us by the time she walks back into the room ten minutes later, her eyes widening and—if I'm not mistaken—her jaw tensing the moment she sees what I've done.

"I think we need to talk," she says, stopping a few feet away from me.

Narrowing my eyes at her, I tilt my head and turn to face her. "Sit down, relax."

"I think it's probably better if I stand for this." Now *that* gets my attention. My spidey senses are tingling, telling me that something's definitely not right here.

She studies me, her eyes roaming over my chest, dropping to my hips, my legs, then returning back to my face. It's then I notice her teeth sinking into her bottom lip—and not in that sexy way I love either.

"Sweetness, what's wr—"

"You don't have to do this anymore."

"What?" I ask, jerking my head back.

"This," she says, waving one hand between us. "If you're here because of some misconceived belief that Brody needs a father, then I think it's better that we end this now. I have real feelings for you and if I'm more invested in this than you are, I think it's better to protect myself now than let myself be the desperate horny single mom that scratches an itch."

One minute we're in the living room having a silent standoff. The next, I've hoisted Amy over my shoulder and I'm carrying her down the hallway in the direction of her bedroom.

Fuck waiting any longer. My patience has been misconstrued as disinterest and there's no way I'm letting the woman I'm going to spend the rest of my life with think I don't want her when nothing could be further from the truth.

"Put me down," she gasps.

"Not gonna happen," I growl.

"Put. Me. Down. Thomas," she stage whispers angrily, almost shrieking.

"Give it up, sweetness. I needed to shut you up."

"I *what?*"

"You heard me."

"You're a Neanderthal. You just . . . *carried* me."

"And you're clueless."

"What?" she splutters before I send her flying through the air, landing on her back on the mattress.

She lifts up, quickly bracing herself on her elbows, glaring at me. If looks could kill, I'd be in mortal danger right now.

"I'm not fucking clueless."

My lips twitch, and I tilt my head, my eyes soft and lazy on her. "Sweetness, you think I'm here because I'm so desperate to get laid that I've targeted the . . . what did you call yourself? The 'desperate horny single mom' who'll take whatever she can get.' And I'm with you because of some deep-seated abandonment issues? Am I right?"

"Yes," she shouts. "Why else would you be here when you've known me for years and never—not once—given me a second look. In fact, you shot me straight to the friend-zone back in the bar all those months ago and until recently, showed no interest at all."

I grit my teeth in frustration because she should know exactly why I didn't try anything back then.

I remember the night vividly. How we talked for over two hours after Michelle threw her drink at me, how Amy kept pouring the drinks so I could drown my sorrows after two weeks of telling women I'd been with that I might have given them an STD—or worse still—that they might've given it to me. Then how she drove me home after closing and even walked my stumbling frame to the front door where Cade was waiting to take over.

"You think I've been waiting because I'm not interested?"

"I don't know," she says, her anger disappearing. She stares at me and I swear I can see her processing my words. "I thought we were moving forward a few weeks ago but then we never get further than second base. You said the next woman you slept with would be the one, so I kinda thought that maybe . . ." She averts her eyes and I watch her chest rise and fall as if she's bracing herself for whatever she's about to say next. "I may have just had a baby but I've been physically ready since my six-week post-natal checkup. I've been emotionally ready for at least a month."

A month. A fucking *month.*

"I wanted things to be perfect," I say, meaning every word but definitely feeling like a prized idiot. "I'd organized a sleep-over for Brody with Gareth and Kristy next week. We were going to have twenty-four hours of uninterrupted adult time at my apartment."

Her eyes widen and the room goes deathly quiet before she suddenly bursts out laughing, like rolling around on the bed kind of laughing. When she calms down she lifts herself on her elbows again to look at me. "All the while, I've been going through batteries like a hooker goes through condoms, and biding my time, hoping like hell you'll make a move so I don't have to invest in sex toy stock options." My mouth drops open and it crosses my mind that I might be dreaming. Surely this amazing woman in front of me can't be real.

Then again, if this is a dream, I don't ever want to wake up.

"Life isn't perfect, Thomas. It has moments where it

comes really freaking close but we both know—from experience—there are times when it's so far from ideal it's ridiculous. I had a drunken one-night stand and ended up pregnant. You got an STD and don't know who from." She gets off the mattress and closes the distance between us. I open my mouth but snap it shut when she puts her hands on my abs and glides them up my chest, over my neck, and only stopping to cup my jaw. It takes every ounce of control I have just to hold on to her hips and not throw her back on the bed. "I love that you wanted our first time to be perfect but in waiting to give me that, it allowed all of my hidden insecurities and perceived inadequacies as a woman to come rushing to the surface and spew out of my mouth." She pulls my face down to brush her lips against mine. "Us girls have our moments of crazy, the measure of a man is how well he copes with them."

"If that was your crazy, baby, I know exactly how I'm gonna handle you. Case in point. I'm about to lay you down, strip you naked and take my time making sure you have no doubt whatsoever just how much I want you."

Her breath hitches and her body trembles against mine. She's with me in this moment. She's totally fucking on board with everything that's about to happen.

Halle-fucking-lujah.

I walk her backward, pushing on her hips at the same time I'm dropping my mouth to hers and kissing her like there's no tomorrow.

I don't want to ever stop kissing this woman. And tonight I'm going to take her to bed and make her mine in every way possible, reiterating the truth of my words as I touch, taste, and feel every single inch of her body.

Her knees hit the bed just as I delve my tongue between her lips, waging a war both of us want to win.

I throw my arm out to brace myself on the mattress, pressing my body into hers so she can feel how much I want her.

I'm desperate with the need to bury myself inside her but I know I need to take my time with her first. It's been a while for both of us. I want it to be good for her because she's going to be the first and last woman I make love to. It's not something I can fuck up.

Just the thought has me sporting the world's first granite erection. I'm harder than I've ever been and know that I'm a hair's breadth away from ending the party before it's even begun, something that would *not* be cool.

"Touch me," she says, murmuring against my lips as her hands start to roam, running over my back, my shoulders, my arms, and everywhere else she can reach.

So I do. I pour everything I feel for her into that kiss. I run my hand down her chest to cup her breast, loving the way she arches her back to press further into me.

Drifting my lips down her jaw, I drag my tongue along her skin as I dip my fingers beneath her top and lift it up, exposing her white lace bra.

She grabs the fabric and rips it off over her head, throwing it to the floor then bringing her hands around my waist to pull my shirt up. I follow her lead and toss it aside, my mind solely focused on getting my mouth back where I really want it to be.

Her fingers tangle in my hair, tightening when I tug her bra down and wrap my lips around her nipple, sucking it into my mouth and laving it with my tongue.

I shift my weight to the side, easing the pressure on my

dick as I try to fight the urge to grind against her. Moving my hand down her body, I rub the palm of my hand against her clit, cursing the layers between us.

She pulls my head back up to hers, moaning into my mouth with every stroke of my hand.

"Too many clothes," she groans, grinding her pelvis into my hand.

I release her nipple and move back to kiss her, my lips smashing against hers. It's not a gentle coaxing kiss. It's an 'I need to swallow you whole' kind of kiss.

Requiring oxygen, I rest my forehead against hers, breathing her in and trying to calm down so this party doesn't end prematurely. I brace my hands on the mattress and lean my body over, pressing into her.

I lift up and look down, loving her flushed cheeks, hooded eyes and swollen mouth.

"How are you doing, sweetness?" I ask as I thrust my hips against her.

"God, that feels good."

"You want more of that?"

"Yes, but minus the pants and underwear," she says with a sexy grin.

"Deal." I push off the bed and stand in front of her, my hands going to my belt. I must say it's fucking hot watching her eyes roam over me, especially my waist and everything that's going on below it.

"Are you gonna give me a show?" she asks with a sly smile.

"Do you want a show?"

"I think you *want* to give me a show."

"If I'm getting naked, so are you."

"I seem to recall you telling me *you* were going to strip me down . . ." She lifts a hand to her mouth, mindlessly rubbing her thumb along her bottom lip.

"Jesus," I groan, shucking my pants and boxers off in one swift tug before moving over her again and brushing my lips against hers, needing another taste.

Actually, I need more than just a taste. I need to drown in her, lose myself completely in *her*.

I run a hand behind her back, thankful when she arches up to give me room as I unclasp her bra—well, it takes a few goes because *hello,* out of practice here—and toss it to the floor with the rest of our clothes.

Her breasts are beautiful, so full and round and fucking perfect, so much so I can't drag my eyes off them. Voodoo boobs. If ever a thing existed, then Amy would be their master and keeper.

"I'll warn you now, the girls might leak a bit if I . . . you know . . ."

That breaks the spell. I lift my chin to her face, meeting her dancing eyes with no doubt wide ones.

"Are you serious?"

"Yep," she says with a wicked grin.

"And you'd know this how?" She covers her face with her arm but I don't miss her bright red cheeks.

Chuckling, I gently grab her wrist and move her arm away and lower my mouth to her ear. "Sweetness, with what we're about to do, and everything we're hopefully going to do, there's going to be nothing between us."

I move back when she turns toward me, our gazes meeting again. "I *want* to know what turns you on . . ." Dipping my head, I brush my lips against her. "I *need* to know what makes you so hot you can barely breathe . . ." I nip the corner of her mouth then soothe the sting with a swipe of the tip of my tongue. "And I definitely need to know it was me you were thinking about when you touched yourself and made yourself leak."

I lose every train of thought when she grabs hold of my shoulders, hooks her leg around my calf and flips me over onto my back before attacking my mouth with renewed hunger.

There's something to be said about a woman taking control to get what she wants, and there's no doubt in my mind that Amy wants me.

I stop holding back, I give as good as I get, kissing, nipping, licking, sucking, everything and everywhere, all of me and all of her, switching positions so she's on her back again with my body against hers.

When her hands leave me to get her jeans off, I shift back and straddle her thighs, helping her wiggle out of her pants while taking the availed opportunity to let my hands roam over her skin.

The moment we're both naked, there's absolutely nothing that can stop us. I smash my mouth against hers, our teeth clashing as the hunger between us reaches a breaking point.

I run my mouth down her body again, this time with only one goal in mind, to drive her absolutely insane and get that taste of her I've been craving for months on my tongue.

The moment I sweep my tongue against her clit, she cries out. I lift my eyes to watch her, grinning against her skin when she grabs a pillow and shoves it over her face to muffle the sounds she has no control over.

It's then I lose myself in her, one hand gripping her hip, the fingers of the other delving inside her, feeling her clamp around me the more I work her up.

She clasps my shoulders, pulling me away. When I move over her again she grabs hold of my face and kisses me, the smell and taste of her surrounding us.

"Condom, top drawer," she mutters, the words caressing my lips with every breath.

I lift my head and quirk a brow, a sly grin playing at my mouth. "Need I ask?"

She shakes her head, smiling back at me. "They're from BB, *before* Brody."

I kiss her hard and fast before lifting up and reaching over to her bedside table, jerking the handle and rummaging inside, pulling my hand out when I find purchase on a welcome foil packet.

Standing up in front of her, I quickly rip the packaging, rolling the rubber down just as Amy's fingers join mine to finish the job.

"Any more of that, and this party will be over before we've even begun."

"Oh, I don't doubt it," she says with a laugh. "I think we're both going to be quick triggers first time around." She winks and lies back down, holding her arms open for me to join her.

I stand there and peruse her naked form laid out before me, a vision I've fantasized about for months and months.

"You're beautiful."

"And you're wasting time," she says huskily. Four words that spur me on as she no doubt intended.

I move onto the bed, cupping her breasts in my hands on my way down, pushing them together and rolling my tongue over one nipple and then the other.

Bracing my forearms on either side of her, I grind my hips against hers, running my cock between her legs and groaning at the feeling.

She tangles her fingers in my hair and again holds her lips to mine. "I need you inside me, Thomas. Make me your last."

And I'm done for. I pull back and with our eyes locked, I slowly push inside her, loving the way her eyelids flutter closed the moment I'm all the way in.

Fuck, there's nothing like the feel of her. Absolutely fucking *nothing* like having my cock inside of Amy.

I already feel the tell-tale pressure at the base of my spine and I know there's no way I'm going to last as long as Amy deserves. That doesn't mean I can't make it good for her first though.

Bringing a hand between us, I rub my thumb over her clit just as our mouths meet in a frenzied kiss, her grip on my head tightening as she thrusts her hips up against mine as if to urge me on.

In what feels like moments later, but I'm sure is at least a few minutes—I hope anyway—Amy clenches around my cock, her movements becoming frantic as she claws at my hair, her mouth devouring me whole as I hammer into her harder and faster, wanting to come with her.

When she whimpers against my lips I lose hold of the last scrap of control I have and let go, thrusting into her twice more as I empty myself into her, knowing that there's no way I can ever let this woman go.

I brush my lips against hers, our breaths coming in hard and fast pants as we come down from the high of climax. "This is it now, sweetness. Us against the world."

She smiles against my skin, her eyes locked with mine. "I

love you."

"That's good because I fucking love you too."

She giggles and runs her hands up my arms, curling over my neck to cup my jaw before she kisses me soft and slow, as if to seal our words and commemorate the moment.

She shifts beneath me, her gaze turning hooded once more.

"So when do I get round two . . ."

I pin her with a heated stare, my dick twitching in anticipation at a repeat performance just as the room is filled with the crackle of static and a quiet cry from the other important person in both our lives over the baby monitor.

"Let's table that for future reference," I say with a grin, kissing her quickly before rolling over and swinging my legs over the side of the bed.

"I can get him," she says, the covers rustling behind my back. I shake my head and look over my shoulder at her. "I just need to get a towel to clean up since my boobs decided to give us a milk bath." I chuckle at that, not caring one bit that she leaked. In fact, the taste I got when I was paying close attention to her gorgeous breasts is not something I'll forget in a hurry.

"You stay there, I'll get him." The expression on her face is one I won't forget anytime soon.

Something tells me I earned brownie points with that one.

"Okay," she whispers.

It's not until I'm dressed and almost in the hall that she speaks again.

"Thomas?" I stop in the doorway and turn toward her.

"Yeah, sweetness."

"I'm glad I'm your last because that means you're mine too. And I wouldn't want it any other way."

15

TWO MONTHS LATER

Amy

"I love your bath. I don't think I ever want to leave," I sigh, leaning my weight into Thomas behind me.

"Glad you like it," he murmurs, his hands continuing their exploration of my body, wherever he can reach.

Suffice to say, life has been rather good since Thomas and I sealed the deal that night two months ago. One, I got over myself and my insecurities about Thomas and the reasons why he was with us, and two, things between Thomas and I have been nothing short of perfection. I get those belly whooshes on a daily basis when he's around and I've loved being able to share Brody's milestones with him.

I have that family unit I wanted for Brody. The one I'd imagined creating with Thomas months ago when he ensconced himself in our lives.

And right now, I'm in the middle of very enjoyable adult time with Thomas in his claw-footed tub.

"Lean forward," he whispers in my ear. I quiver at the feel of his breath against the damp skin of my neck.

Doing as asked, I move so my boobs are almost touching my knees, conveniently moving my ass up against his hard cock. That thought is waylaid when a soft loofah slowly glides across my shoulder blades and down my spine.

What pleases me more is the wandering hand sliding up my side and curling around my breast.

He brushes his lips against the curve of my neck. "I told you baths are fun."

"Are you okay with going to dinner at Sean and Sam's next week?" I ask, arching my back into him.

"Of course. Why wouldn't I be?"

"I just wanted to check with you, that's all. It's what couples do."

He wraps his arm around my shoulders and tilts my face so I'm looking straight at him. "I like that," he says with a bright smile.

Tilting my head, I scrunch my nose. "You like what?"

"Us doing normal, everyday couple things."

I giggle and lean back into him, smiling to myself when he starts washing me again, this time paying particular attention to my highly sensitive—and very inviting—body parts.

"You do know that we've been doing lots of everyday normal couple things for quite a while now. In fact, you were doing my laundry and bringing me food before the concept of us as a couple was even a possibility."

"Don't think for one second that we were ever *not* a possibility, sweetness."

Needing more contact, more *everything* from Thomas, I roll over, sloshing water all over the bathroom floor but not giving one shit about it in that moment.

I rest my forearms on his chest and look up, not missing

the way his eyes heat as they scan the unadulterated view he's now getting of my ass peeking out of the water. "Who would've thought you'd be so organized to arrange a 'bath' date."

"An adult bath date with you . . . naked . . ."

"And wet . . ."

"That too."

"And even arranging a portable crib for Brody. You're quite the problem solver aren't you? A date with a baby in the bath minus the baby."

"Babies don't get adult bath time. That's a special treat for sexy MILFs. We're just lucky he's still happy having naps."

I tilt my head. "You often have MILFs in your bath?"

He drops his head back and laughs before returning his amused gaze to me. "Nope, you're definitely the first."

"I wouldn't say I'm a MILF though, more a MIAF." His brows furrow and he looks adorably puzzled.

His lips slowly morph into a wicked grin. "A mom I'm about to fuck?"

"Let's see, shall we?" I rise up and kiss him, delving my tongue between his parted lips as his hands run down to my ass, his fingers biting into my skin.

I begin to rock my hips against his, jolts of pleasure scoring through me with every slide and glide.

"Fuck," he groans as I push myself so my breasts are right there in his line of sight. Wrapping his big hand beneath one, he drops his head forward, dragging his lips across the sensitive skin before circling my pert nipple with the tip of his tongue.

"I think . . . I'm gonna love . . . adult bath time . . ." I whimper as he sets out to drive me wild and send me soaring.

He runs his fingers down my body before delving between my legs and stroking his thumb over my clit in dizzying circles while easing two fingers inside of me.

With trembling legs, I feel my climax advancing like a category five hurricane. "Thomas . . ." I moan, unable to verbalize anything else other than moans and whimpers. His hand cups my jaw and he crushes his lips against mine, swallowing my cries as I fall over the edge, my hips thrusting against his hand as he makes sure I ride the wave right to the end.

Not nearly satisfied, I move up to straddle him, his hands gripping my hips and holding me in place as I roll my hips along the length of his cock, earning a gratifying growl in return.

I run my hands over his chest, following them with my body until my breasts are pressing against him and my mouth is within licking distance of his neck.

"Now it's your turn," I whisper before nipping his jaw.

"No . . . condom," he stutters, his fingers biting into my skin as he grips my ass, urging me to continue rocking against him. Water splashes over and around us and if I had the ability to think of anything else other than getting him inside me, I'd probably worry about flooding his bathroom floor. Scratch that, *nothing* could get me to care whether water gets everywhere. I'm tunnel-visioned right now with one mission; blow his mind as much as he just blew mine.

I cup his face with my hands and bring my lips down to rest against his. "Am I your last, Thomas?"

"Fuck yeah you are," he growls.

"And would you ever give me anything other than you?"

"Never."

"Then we don't need condoms because I'm on birth control." I lift my head and look him dead in the eye. "And I trust you."

"Jesus," he curses before he sits up, wraps an arm around my waist taking my hips with him. His spare hand reaches between us, giving a delicious stroke of my clit on the way past before he grips the base of his cock, positions himself, then drives me down just as he thrusts up, both of us groaning in complete and utter bliss before I set out to ride him like a prized bull.

At last count, we share five orgasms in that bath—four of mine to Thomas's one—leaving me with a goofy grin on my face when he finally lets me succumb to exhaustion flat on my face on his bed.

———

It's Sunday night and we're standing at the door of Sean and Sam's two level monstrosity of a house in North Center. I remember when Sean first showed me the listing two years ago and despite being here many times since, I still can't get over the beauty of it.

There are five bedrooms, a wall of floor to ceiling windows lining the living area of the house, beautiful mahogany wide plank floors and granite countertops in what must be the most state-of-the-art kitchen I've ever seen. It screams class, it screams elegance, but most importantly, there's no mistaking that this is a family home.

A family home with three rather rambunctious kids that I love almost as much as Brody.

Having pressed the doorbell, we're met a minute later by Sean and Sam's seven-year-old daughter Megan.

She stands there staring at us, not saying a word as she moves her eyes from me to Thomas, before glaring at him as she looks him down from head to toe.

"Hey, Megan," I say cheerfully, confused by her reaction. "Can we come in? We're here to have dinner with you guys."

"Why's Thomas here?" she asks, hands on her hips in the perfect haughty woman pose—a pint-sized one.

"He's my boyfriend now, Megan." She tilts her head and narrows her eyes on where Thomas's fingers are entwined with mine.

"I thought Uncle Ryan was your boyfriend?"

I stop breathing. Yep. That's me, killed by shock from a seven-year-old's need to know everything—or ability to know far more than she should.

I go to open my mouth to say some something—okay anything—when I'm saved by Sam.

"Megan, are you going to let them in or interrogate them at the door?" she calls out, her voice thankfully getting closer with every word.

I sneak a side glance at Thomas who seems confused with Megan's announcement going by his bunched brow.

"Why are you with my Aunt Amy?" she looks him up and down again. "And *my* Brody. He's mine, not yours. You can't have him."

Looks like someone had a side of sass with her Wheaties this morning.

"Should we come inside so you can play with Brody?" I ask, really hoping the guard dog seven-year-old will stand down and let us in.

"Megan, stop the doorstep interrogation and let our guests in. You don't want Brody to get cold, do you?"

"Thomas is holding *my* Brody. Can he stay outside?"

"Megan Helen Miller, you better step aside now," Sam says, turning the corner and coming into view.

"She can't stick me in jail because I'm only seven. I looked it up and mommies can't arrest their own daughters," Megan whispers. She's *definitely* way too clever for her own good.

Sam taps her daughter on her shoulder, the little girl's eyes growing wide as it hits her that her mom just heard everything she said. Sam bends down so her mouth is by Megan's ear. "I'm thinking you should go see what your brother is doing in your room since the last thing I saw was your *favorite* stuffed animal getting dragged along the floor."

With a frustrated girly squeak, Megan turns on her heels and quickly runs out of sight as Sam stands up straight and steps to the side. "Please excuse my daughter, she has good intentions however they seem to come out with a healthy dose of diva attitude at the moment," she says with a laugh.

"She's definitely strong-willed," Thomas adds.

"Wonder where she gets that from," Sean says, coming up behind his wife, their youngest daughter Alex on his hip. So different from that alpha vibe he gives off at the club, that's for sure.

Can you imagine the nerves I felt the day I turned up for my job interview with him and I'm met by this tall, ridiculously handsome, and commandingly-persuasive man? Don't get me wrong, when it comes to selling myself, I've never lacked self-confidence. But in the face of Sean Miller with his piercing blue eyes that I swore could see straight through me, I was shaking in my knee-high boots.

Thankfully for me—and for him if I must say so myself—I got the job, and the rest, as they say, is history. Now, we're more than just employee and boss. He's family, and Sam and the kids are too.

"Your daughter is going to give you guys a run for your money in the next ten years," Thomas says, closing the front door behind us as we finally make it inside.

"What do you mean? She's been keeping us on our toes since the moment she could talk," Sam replies with a laugh. "Don't you remember the crop incident?"

Sean chuckles from in front of us as he leads us into the living area, where Megan is wrestling a toy from her brother TJ's little hands.

"Mee-han," little Alex says, wriggling in Sean's arms until he lets her go. The minute her feet hit the ground she's off to join the scrummage with her siblings.

I smile as I watch them, imagining what life would be like with three kids. Picturing what any children Thomas and I might have could look like. What was once a pipe dream is now more probable than possible as our relationship seems to become more and more permanent as every day passes.

"Should we leave Brody to sleep?" the man in question asks from beside me, knocking me from my thoughts.

I look down at my peacefully sleeping son, calculating the likelihood of him going down for the night later. "We should probably wake him. If I nurse him now, he can have some tummy time and he should be good to go when we leave."

"Sounds like a plan, sweetness." He leans in to kiss my lips and rub his nose against the side of mine before turning to Sam. "Do you mind if I change him in the living room? I'm just going to get him up."

"Not a problem. I'll go grab you a towel."

I watch this whole scene play out and honestly wonder how I got so lucky. Good friends and family, an awesome son, an *amazing* boyfriend, and I realize that for the first time in a long time I'm truly happy.

"Penny for your thoughts?" Sean asks from the kitchen. I make my way over to him and take a seat at the boat-sized kitchen island.

He watches me like I'm an animal rarely seen in the wild and the longer he does it, the more disconcerted I become.

"What?"

"I like you like this."

"Like what?" I tilt my head and narrow my eyes at him.

"Content. Comfortable. Just . . . you."

"Now what does *that* mean?" I ask as I hear happy Brody squeals from the other side of the monstrosity that is Sean's house.

Sean puts his hand on the counter and leans forward, pinning me in place with his 'now listen here' stare. "Amy, it means that I'm happy that you're happy. I'm over the fucking moon. You deserve everything you've got right now *and* more."

I shake my head at him, knowing that he's slipped into the big brother role he plays oh so well.

He looks over my shoulder as Thomas and Sam's voices get closer. "Can we talk later?" he asks, dropping his voice to a low whisper.

"About . . . ?" I raise a brow, confused as to why he's being secretive.

"Just make sure we talk before you leave tonight." *Alrighty then.*

"Okay . . ." I lean toward him, whispering back, "why are we whispering?"

He shakes his head and scowls, trying his 'I mean business' look on me even though he knows it never works.

Standing up straight, he grins at Sam as she rounds the island and slides her arm around his waist. "At least my nasty dom looks work on you."

"Or I let you *think* they work on me."

Sean's head jerks back as he regards his wife, his brows almost hitting his hairline. "I think we'll test this theory out later." Sam blushes—freaking *blushes*—her ice queen cop persona nowhere to be seen.

Thomas wraps his arms around me and I lean back into him.

"How's Brody?"

"He's good. I changed his diaper and he's lying under a play gym Sam set up for him."

"Helps that our kids think he's a new toy to play with," Sean adds, his grin growing when Thomas's arms tighten around me as I start to get up.

"I just want to—"

"He's fine, Amz. *Relax,*" Thomas says in my ear, his warm breath sending a delicious tremble down to my happily serviced but now-in-need-of-more-attention lady parts.

"Dinner should be ready in about fifteen minutes if that's okay," Sam announces. "That'll give you guys enough time to wrangle the kids and get them up to the table." By the time she's finished, she's looking up at her smirking husband, the smart bastard not missing the instruction.

"You're lucky I love you," Sean murmurs, dipping his head to kiss his wife's mouth. "We've been told, Thomas. Maybe this will give you practice for when you guys have your own herd of kids."

Thomas kisses my temple, giving me a chance to hide my reaction to the kid comment while taking another hit of his swoon-inducing aftershave. Whatever it is, I want to bathe in it and spray it in every corner of my house so I can forever remain in a Thomas fog.

When I told him that earlier tonight when he emerged from my bathroom, he shook his head at me like I was a loon and chuckled as he dropped his towel and shucked his pants on.

Of course, I wasn't laughing at Thomas walking around my bed naked as the day he was born, my mind was focused on something else entirely; a something that obviously he knew I was looking at and he decided to put on a show for me, a command performance in fact.

"You look happy," Sam says from the stove top where she's stirring something delicious smelling in a pot.

"That's because I am."

"Has Ryan called you?" she asks, never being one to beat around the bush. Turning to face me, her eyes are now soft, but inquisitive.

Ryan is Sean's brother. Also, the former bar manager at Throb who I had the drunken late night romp with approximately sixteen months ago, resulting in my gorgeous Brody.

"I wasn't expecting him to. He made himself pretty clear when I told him I was pregnant, then again when he walked away, never to be seen or heard from again."

"He's in town again. He turned up on our doorstep a few days ago."

Well, fuck.

"Is he . . ."

"Yes, he's sober and going to GA and AA meetings. He's got a sponsor too. He says he's been sober for twelve months now."

"That's good, Sam. But you'll have to forgive me if I'm not rushing out for balloons and streamers to celebrate his return." I take a deep breath, trying to relieve the tension in my shoulders that has my head feeling like it's in a vise.

"I know, Amz, and Sean knows that too. But Ryan asked about you and about the baby, and I think he wants to talk to you."

My body jerks back like I've been hit, the stool I'm sitting on scraping back against the tiles as I get to my feet.

"Oh no. *Hell* no."

"Amy . . ."

"No, Sam. He doesn't get to run away from responsibility for something we *both* did, then try and walk back in almost sixteen months later."

"I'm not sure he's—"

"I mean, Brody's six months old for Christ's sake. Where was Ryan when his son was born? Where was he when Brody was sick at two months old?" I heave in a breath, needing more oxygen before I continue my tirade. "My son doesn't need another father figure, especially not a biological parent who didn't stand up when he should've. He's got Thomas. He's the only dad he needs." My voice is a near shout at this stage and just my luck, it's the exact moment that Sean emerges from the hallway followed by three smiling and laughing children, with Thomas and Brody coming up in the rear.

The expression on both of the men's faces morphs into concern when they see my face, my eyes feeling like they're going to pop out of my head from the pressure of it all.

"Amz?" Thomas asks, coming straight to me. "What's wrong?"

"It's nothing," I say, letting out the breath I didn't know I was holding.

"Considering I've only heard you speak like that one other time and that was when you were trying to end things with me because you thought you were a pity screw, I know for a fact that you're lying to me right now."

I burrow my face in his chest, blinking rapidly to stop the tears from coming when his strong arms pull me in close.

It's not that I'm sad, it's that I'm so freaking mad I'm close to losing it.

My life is so good right now, why would I want anything—or anyone—to come in and fuck with my perfectly balanced scales.

I feel a tiny fist grab a clump of hair and I turn my head to be met with the curious blue eyes of Brody. That's all I get to see though as he soon dives right on in, giving me a slobbery attempt at a cheek kiss that actually gets my nose. I snort as Thomas pulls back just a little and meets my eyes.

"You know I'm going to make you tell me, right?"

I sigh and nod. "Yeah, but let's enjoy tonight. I'm hungry and dinner smells amazing."

"I need to know you're okay, sweetness." His eyes are so soft, his concern obvious.

"I'm okay," I whisper just as my head is tugged sideways by my hair thanks to my son. "And I think this little guy wants his dinner too."

Moving back, Thomas hands Brody over to me, watching me closely as he does it.

I look over at Sean who is leaning against the wall with his arms and ankles crossed, his piercing gaze pinned on me.

I quirk a brow at him, a silent challenge for him to bring up the subject of his brother again. He yields first—a *very* rare occurrence indeed—and gives a quick jerk of his head. I shoot a knowing smirk his way which earns a twitch of his lips.

Work wife—one, alpha dom boss—zero. Now I've just gotta deal with Thomas later and I'll be two and oh for the night.

16

Thomas

Amy is noticeably quiet on the drive home from Sean's house.

I may have missed the start of her talk with Sam but I sure as shit didn't miss the end when she said I'm the only dad Brody needs. That felt fucking fantastic and would have been a Hallmark moment had it not been for the revelation that Ryan Miller is Brody's father.

I was so conflicted, wanting to fist pump the air with one hand while using the other to hunt Ryan down and knock him out.

But Amy needed me to keep my cool, so I did. I wanted to be the calm in her storm and as always, as soon as I had her cocooned in my arms, she sagged into me. It helped that Brody decided in that moment to be cute and try and suck her face off.

Never have I ever felt more protective of the two of them than I did in that moment.

Never have I felt more pride in my life either.

"Brodz did really well tonight."

"Yeah." Her tone is flat and I can tell she's distracted.

"Amz, I think we should—"

She turns her head and rests her cheek on the headrest, her eyes set on me. "I love you." Three words that never fail to make me feel like a fucking superhero.

I reach my hand over and gently squeeze her leg. "I could hear you say that to me every day for the rest of my life and it would still make me feel invincible."

"I'll remember that." Comfortable silence stretches between us and it's not until a few minutes have passed that Amy speaks again. "I want to talk about it but I want to do it with your arms around me."

"Okay, sweetness. That I can definitely do."

And that was that.

Now we're on Amy's couch, lying side by side with our legs entwined, my fingers playing mindlessly with a strand of her hair having just been given the full story of Ryan Miller and his lack of involvement with Amy and in turn, Brody.

"Are you mad at me?" Her voice is quiet, almost timid, and very un-Amy like. My head jerks at her question. How can she think that?

"I've got absolutely no reason to be mad at you. It's not like you were purposefully not telling me he was Brody's father. Ryan, on the other hand, is a different story."

"Why? I didn't think you knew him?"

"I only met him a few times but knowing that he walked away from you guys has me fighting the urge to hunt him down, kick his ass then sterilize him."

She giggles and rests her forehead against mine. "I think that's the first stage."

"Why's that?"

"I wanted to do the same thing when he told me he couldn't deal with me being pregnant. He'd fallen off the wagon for the millionth time the night we hooked up. And that's all it was, a drunken hookup. Despite what Megan said tonight, Ryan and I were never anything more than colleagues. I want you to know that."

I run my hand over her hair, down her back and up again. "It's okay, sweetness."

"I'm sorry I got so animated at Sean's place. I felt blind-sided, so I reacted. I knew he'd come back at some stage but I didn't think he'd ask about either of us."

"You were a mama bear protecting her cub. It's totally understandable." She inches her hands under my tee, sliding her fingers against my skin. There's no intent in her actions, it's more comfort than anything else.

"I don't know how I should feel. I mean, he's Brody's father, he has rights, I know that, it's just—"

"He has no fucking rights," I growl through gritted teeth. "He gave everything up when he walked away."

"It was the best thing for everyone involved."

"It was the best thing for *Ryan.* Everything he's done was about Ryan and *only* Ryan. If you're man enough to have sex, you're man enough to face up to the consequences if there are any."

Her hands rub over my pecs before she curves her fingers around my shoulders. "Like you did?"

She gets me, she totally fucking gets me. Can she be more

perfect? Never have I been surer of the fact that Amy was *meant* to be my last than right now.

I kiss her because right now I *need* to kiss her. I touch my lips to hers gently, knowing this isn't one of those 'leading into something' kisses. No, it's an expression of emotion, of feeling, a need to have a physical connection to the woman I love during what I know must be a confusing time for her.

"Yeah, I did the crime, I did my time." I try not to laugh—I really do—but the fact that my 'time' involved getting a swab stick stuck down places no man wants a swab stick to go and telling a few very disgruntled women that I had an STD, is actually quite funny. At the time it wasn't, but now it definitely is.

When Amy's body starts to shake against mine, and a soft snort escapes her lips, I give up the ghost and start chuckling quietly too.

By the time we get that out of our system, I decide it's time to make sure she's really okay.

I pull back slightly and bring my arms between us, cupping her cheeks to ensure I have her full intention.

"Now tell me the truth, how are you really feeling?" Her eyes go from wary to gentle as she leans her face into my touch.

"I'm indifferent when it comes to him not supporting me but when it comes to Brody, I'm like you said, a mama bear. An *angry* mama bear who needs to protect everyone she loves. Not just Brody but you too."

"Why me?"

"Because you are just as much a part of this family as I am. You're the one who's been here for me and for Brody since the day he was born."

"I wasn't much for you before that," I concede.

"We weren't like that before Lucky Charms and dirty grocery store floors." She grins at me, and I kiss her hard and fast, wiping the smile off her face and leaving her struggling to breathe by the end of it.

"You may not have been much to me back then, but you're everything to us now."

17

Amy

"You look well and truly fucked," Mia announces the minute I open my front door on Monday night for our *Bachelorette* viewing party this time. Dani and Abi follow closely behind her.

"Take that back," I reply, pointing my finger at Mia. "Oh and hi, how are you? I'm great, thanks for asking." She smirks at me but doesn't greet me like any other normal human being would.

"Nope," she replies, shaking her head. "You have crazy sex hair and lips that say you've been sucking cock like a lollipop. You've totally been riding the Thomas train. Did he at least make you toot? Is he still here? I'll ask the man himself if you won't tell me."

"Mia!" Dani gasps as she drops down to the floor to pick Brody up from his mat where he's sitting up happily bashing a drum Thomas bought him last week. "Stop it!"

"Well trains don't squirt so toot is an acceptable analogy," Abi adds, helpfully as they all make themselves comfortable in the living room. My stepmom Kristy emerges from the kitchen, wine bottle and a plate of snacks in hand.

"Am I wrong?" Mia says, not giving up. When both Abi and Dani shake their heads, agreeing with her, she turns her attention back to me. "So sit down and tell us all about it. Is he a grower or a shower? Because in my mind he just *has* to be packing down there. He's way too charming and cocky to be small. And let's be honest, after waiting so long between drinks, it wouldn't be right for you to get one that doesn't touch the sides."

"Mia!" Dani gasps while Abi just laughs her ass off.

"What? I can't be the only one that's curious? It's like she's been tied to the bed as his sex slave the last few months. They both barely come up for air and I'm not the only one who's noticed."

When I finally stop laughing because honestly, there's nobody else who puts things quite the way Mia does, I shoot her a knowing wink.

"A lady never tells."

"You haven't been anything close to a lady since the moment you were born. Spill, woman," Mia presses. I look at Kristy whose eyes are dancing with amusement. Definitely no sign of this being TMI for her. Well, it would be TMI for anybody other than these women. The only other person I know that has no filter and holds nothing back is Mac.

"I'm sorry you feel neglected. Should I schedule you in my calendar in between sessions?"

"I think you should," Mia replies, her lips twitching as she struggles to hold back a giggle.

"Add me in too," Abi says with a knowing grin. I turn my attention to Dani.

"You too?" I quirk a brow, this whole conversation turning almost farcical.

"Nope. I'm good. Besides, I'm too busy practicing making one of these beautiful things," she says, turning her attention to a yawning Brody in her lap.

I get up and walk over to her. "I think my boy needs a final feeding and then I'll put him down for the night."

Dani's eyes go to my boobs before she looks back up at my face. "That still fascinates me. I've seen Zoe, Mia and Kate nurse their babies but the whole thing is truly amazing. And your rack is pretty damn impressive, Amz."

I feel my cheeks heat and I bite my lip to hold back laughter.

"Dani, did you really just tell Amy that she has a good rack?" Abi asks, snickering away in the corner of the room.

"Just stating facts."

"As you do," Mia mutters, giving her sister the side-eye.

"So . . ." Kristy says, breaking through what might possibly be the most random conversation we've ever had. "Anyone for more food?"

Halfway through the program, my phone vibrates with a text.

Thomas: I've just made a 'to-do' list for tomorrow and you're on it.

Amy: So I'm slotted right on in there between doing laundry and attending a client meeting?

Thomas: Actually, I've given myself the day off so you're next on the schedule after having a shower and jerking off thinking about you, then driving over to your house to play with Brody, then ravaging you when he has his morning nap.

Amy: What if I already have a mommy-son date and won't be here when you turn up?

Thomas: I could crash the mommy-son date. What do you say?

Amy: Only if I still get the ravaging afterward.

Thomas: That's a given. The only variable in this equation is time. Me + you = guaranteed orgasm or your money back.

Amy: Prostitution is illegal you know.

Thomas: Only if you get caught ;)

Amy: You're incorrigible.

Thomas: And you're so irresistible that I'd willingly take the rap for any lewd acts I'm found guilty of.

Amy: I may need a demonstration of exactly what these lewd acts would be.

Thomas: I think the variable has changed and the equation has turned into multiplication.

Amy: What do you mean?

Thomas: Me + You = orgasms x at least 3.

Amy: That's mighty big talk then, stud.

Thomas: Stud works ;)

Later on in bed, I pick up my phone to send Thomas a goodnight text when I see a message waiting for me from a number I've never seen before.

Unknown: Hi, it's Ryan. I know I'm probably the last person you want to talk to but I think we need to talk.

Checking the time, I make a snap decision—wrong or right, I'm not sure—and call him, knowing full well I won't be able to sleep without knowing what he wants.

I call the number, my heart galloping like a racehorse in my chest as the ringing tone continues to chime in my ear.

"Hey, Amz," Ryan says answering the call.

"Hey." I'm not sure what else to say, I mean. It's not like our last conversation could be described as pleasant.

"Thanks for calling me."

"You're the father of my son."

He doesn't say anything for a long time. So much so, I even pull the phone away from my ear to check that the call is still connected.

"Ryan?" I ask, failing to hide the uncertainty in my voice.

"Yeah, I'm here. It's just surreal hearing myself being called that. It's not exactly something I ever saw in my future."

"Ryan, you've known for fourteen months that you were a father to Brody. And I don't believe that Sean would've held back in giving you updates—even if you didn't want them—whenever you called him."

"I forgot how astute you are."

"I'm also happy, Ryan. I'm settled, Brody's settled, I'm seeing someone who has been in Brody's life since the day he was born and who I regard as the closest thing to a father he'll ever have."

"Sean talked to me about that," he says quietly. "Thomas is a good man from what I remember of him."

"He's the best," I say, thinking of him. Wishing he was here right now instead of staying at Cade's. "But I know you don't want to talk about him."

"Did Sean tell you I'm sober?"

"Sam did. Good for you."

"It's a work in progress. Probably always will be," he says softly.

"Ryan, what did you want to talk to me about?" He sighs down the line and I hear him take a steadying breath.

"This isn't easy for me, Amz."

"Do you think the last six months—hell, since the day I found out I was pregnant—have been easy for me? For any of us? You're not the one who was left to carry a baby for nine months, give birth on the dirty floor of a grocery store, and be the only one here day in, day out while I raised *our* baby alone, Ryan."

"I did what I thought was the right thing for everyone."

"And it was, Ryan, because without doing that, I would never have had the chance to get to know Thomas better, and for him to become one of the most important people in my life."

"I . . . I knew Sean would take care of you both. He promised me he would."

"And he has. Everyone has been amazingly supportive. They're my village and I wouldn't have been able to get through this without them."

"Yes, you would have, because you've always been the strong one. You're one of the most independent and self-sufficient women I've ever met."

"Ryan . . ."

"I wanted to know if you would let me meet my son," he rushes out, making my breath catch, my chest seizing in shock.

Of course he wants to meet him. He has a right to meet him. But do I really want to open that door and the possibility of disappointment further down the line if Ryan relapses? And what about Thomas? How would he feel about all of this? In my eyes, he's more of a father to Brody than anyone else will ever be. I need to take his thoughts and feelings into consideration here. We're in a relationship, a serious one, one that is going places. I have plans—long term plans—for

Thomas, Brody and I and I would never do anything to jeopardize that.

"You do know you just said all of that out loud, right?" he says, chuckling under his breath. "You've always done that. You used to do it behind the bar all the time."

Oh fuck on a crap stick.

"I'm sorry, I'm just—"

"Processing the fact that I'm back, I'm sober, and I'm asking something you never thought you'd have to consider?" he says, sounding way more intuitive than I'd ever expect him to be. I can't hold back my nervous laugh.

"Pretty much."

"Look, Amz. Take a few days to think about it. Right now, I'm not planning on going anywhere. I'm staying with a friend of mine in the city and that's about as far as I've gotten so far. But I don't want to pressure you. I just want to meet the catalyst that led to me turning my life around."

I can't exactly say no now, can I?

"Okay."

"Shouldn't you talk it through with Thomas? Sean said things were serious with you."

Shit, he's right there.

"I'll talk to him tomorrow. When would you want to meet?"

"Would next weekend be too soon? We can meet at the park or something, let Brody run around?"

I giggle at that considering Ryan should know from Sean and Sam's kids that there's no way Brody would be running anywhere at almost seven months old. "He's almost crawling, Ryan, definitely not running yet."

"Oh . . . shit. I'm clueless aren't I?" I smile at that.

"Maybe a little, but you've got less hands-on experience at this baby thing than I do."

"Thank you, Amy. You didn't need to even call me and you still did. I would've totally understood if you never spoke to me again."

"Let's get through this first meeting, Ryan. We're never going to be best friends and I may forgive you but I doubt I'll ever forget, but that doesn't mean I have the right to exclude you from Brody's life. You'll always be his biological father."

"You're a good woman, Amz. Brody and Thomas are lucky to have you."

"That they are," I say with confidence, believing it to be true but only because I'm just as lucky to have the two of them too. "I'll text you about next weekend."

"Sounds good. I'll wait to hear from you. Bye, Amz. And thank you."

"Bye, Ryan."

Ending the call, I flop back down onto my bed and stare up at the ceiling, holding my phone in my hand as I run back over the conversation. It was civil, it wasn't even hard. It was . . . normal.

I guess now all that matters is what Thomas is going to say.

Thomas

"Tell me about Ryan."

Cade's eyes meet mine and I know with that one look that he knows Ryan's back in town. "General fuck-up. Total opposite of Sean. He's like quicksand compared to Sean's steady rock. He left shortly after Amy told him she was pregnant. Hasn't been back since."

"Until now."

He nods before lifting his bottle of Corona to his mouth. "Until now."

"He's a dickless wonder," I grind out.

"He's that, but he's also an addict."

"Was an addict. Apparently he's been sober for a while now."

"And the gambling?"

"What about it?"

"He got himself into a situation a few years ago, almost got Sean arrested. He started going to GA but fell off the so-called wagon so many times. Add in the alcohol, and you can see why I said it was the best thing for everyone when he left."

I nod, taking all of this in. Everyone deserves a second chance but do I really want a man like that in Brody's life? Would Amy? Do I even have a say in the matter?

"We all thought that finding out he was going to be a father would change him but he told Sean that he couldn't deal with the pressure so he left. Literally disappeared the next day."

"He asked about Amy and Brody. I think he might want to meet Brody."

My friend studies me, respect and maybe even pride shining in his eyes as a slow grin curls his lips.

"How does Amy feel about that?" I don't answer that one because I'm not sure Amy knows what she wants right now when it comes to Ryan's involvement in her son's life. All I know is that she wants me in her life and I'm damn well going to make sure I'm there for the two of them.

Cade opens his mouth to say something else but snaps it

shut again before smirking at me. "Good choice. Amy is staunchly independent and I know she hates other people being in her business."

"Yet, I've bulldozed my way in and refused to let her get rid of me."

"She needed a man like that. God knows, Ryan would never have done the right thing by her."

"Well, that's obvious." We fall silent, the low buzz from the TV commentators the only sound in the room.

"Is Ryan going to be a problem for you?" Cade asks. If I wasn't thinking about it then, I definitely am now.

"Is he likely to be a problem?"

"Depends if he has truly sorted his shit out. Amy never wanted a relationship with him. It was never about that for them."

My back goes ramrod straight when I realize where he's going with this conversation. "Dude, I am in no way threatened by him."

"Don't imagine you would be. You're ten times the man he will ever be, but unfortunately, that doesn't change the fact that he's Brody's biological father. Nobody can change that."

That truth sinks in and I focus my attention on the television and the Cubs game that we're supposed to be watching, not sitting here talking about our feelings and shit.

I look over at him and smile. "How about we keep our man cards and never tell the women about this conversation?"

"Best thing you've said all night, other than when you offered to get me another beer out of the fridge. That was definitely a close second," the smart ass replies, finishing his bottle and holding it out for me.

"Yeah, yeah, I get the hint." I stand up and grab his empty, making my way into the kitchen to grab each of us a refill.

"Order a pizza while you're in there, you know where the menus are," he calls out.

"What am I? The house boy of Carsen manor?"

"That would probably involve a loincloth if my wife had anything to say about it, so how about we never speak of that again," he says with a chuckle.

"Now that I agree on."

The next morning I'm at Amy's apartment a little after eight a.m. Closing the front door behind me, I walk in to find Amy sitting cross-legged on the couch in short pajama shorts, a tight white tank that does not hide anything, her chocolate brown hair piled into a messy bun on top of her head, her hands cradling her favorite coffee mug as she dazedly looks out the window.

This sight is not a new one. Amy is in no way a morning person. She takes a good twenty minutes after waking up to become what she calls 'human.' The first night I slept over, I was a little worried about her behavior, wondering if she was regretting sharing a bed with me, even if all we did was sleep. But with every morning I spent here after that, I soon learned that Amy Willis is hell for leather unless she gets her twenty minute wake-up time with a cup of steaming hot coffee.

As soon as the time is up, she's absolutely normal, as if her pre-caffeinated zombie state was a figment of my imagination.

"Is it pre or post-coffee time?"

"Mid," she says sleepily, dropping her head to rest on the

back of the recliner just in time for me to lean down and lay a soft, gentle kiss on her. With one last lick of my tongue against her lips, I lift up slightly to meet her eyes. "Morning, sweetness."

"Morning."

"Fuck you're adorable in the mornings." Moving in front of her, I grab the cup out of her hands and place it on the table. Her growl of annoyance soon morphs into a squeak of surprise the moment I pick her up, turn, and sit her back down in my lap in the chair.

She opens her mouth—no doubt to complain—when I decide that silence may be golden, but showing my girl exactly what she does to me is so much better. So I tangle my fingers in her hair, tip her head and really kiss her good morning, loving the way she melts into me. She wraps her arms around my neck and matches my enthusiasm, that's until she one-ups me and straddles my lap, grinding her hips against mine.

Neither of us take it any further than that, knowing Brody could wake up at any time. There's nothing more frustrating than starting something and getting interrupted during the really good parts—let alone just as we're getting to the great part—even if he's probably the only acceptable reason to stop proceedings.

I ease back, holding her close and dropping my head to brush my lips against her bare shoulder.

"I think I might've found a new cure for my morning-itis."

I lean back in the chair and meet her eyes, resting my hands on her hips. "And what's that?" I ask with a curious smile.

"You." She cups my jaw and kisses me softly again.

I chuckle while running my hands up and down her thighs,

unable to resist touching her. "I'm here to be used and abused at any time, sweetness."

"Such a sweet talker."

"I only speak the truth."

"I know. And I love you for it."

I lean back against the headrest. "You know one of the things I love most about you?"

She tilts her head and moves forward, bracing her hands on my chest. "What's that?"

"You're just you. You've always just been you. You know I'm coming over and I walk in to find you wearing that, looking like that, being unapologetically you, and I love you all the more for it. Even back before we started when I was the cocky jerk not getting any, who loved to rile you up, you were always just you."

She drops her weight against me, fortunately bringing her lips to within a whisper's breath of my own. "Stop being sweet when I can't show you appreciation for it."

I quirk my brow and grin. "What kind of appreciation are we talking here? Because I was only telling you the truth but if there's appreciation being offered, I'm not stupid enough to say no . . ."

Her eyes go half-mast and drop to my mouth before lifting back to meet my gaze. "Let's just say that I'm in the mood to take my time . . ."

I must admit, I do consider risking Brody interrupting us—I am a male after all—but since I've loved every time Amy has 'taken her time' with me, I quickly shelve the idea.

"I need to tell you something," she says, thankfully changing the subject and sitting up again. She purses her lips and her body tenses. I have a feeling she's about to tell me something I'm not gonna like.

"Go for it." I try to reassure her while hiding my own unease.

"Ryan text me last night." My eyes widen but I tamp down that uncomfortable twist in my gut at the mention of Brody's biological father.

"Okay . . ." She watches me—her gaze probing—as she sinks her front teeth into her bottom lip.

"He wants to meet Brody. I suggested next weekend." I nod, my throat going tight.

Why is this affecting me so much? I'm in no way insecure about my relationship with Amy or threatened by Ryan's reappearance. They had a one-night thing, a drunken romp that just happened to create the most amazing baby boy that I think of as my own. I should want this for Brody—I do want this for him—but part of me is uneasy about this whole situation.

On the drive over here, I made the decision not to think about the what-ifs or maybes when it came to Ryan Miller and his intentions. I can't control something that is out of my hands but I can protect the two most important people in my life right now. I need to hold on to that thought and be there for Amy.

She averts her eyes, her hand tensing on my chest.

"Hey," I say, placing my index finger under her chin to make her look at me.

"Will you come with me?" She looks uncertain, her teeth gnawing into her bottom lip like her life depends on it.

"Do you want me there?" *Fuck I hope she does.*

Her eyes widen and her brows go up. "Of course. I need you there."

"Then I'm there. Anything you need, anytime you need it,

I'm here for you, sweetness. I mean that." Her response is to kiss me again, soft and slow, pouring everything into it. It's then the sound of Brody babbling over the baby monitor fills the room, making us both laugh.

"You good?"

"You're here, so of course I am."

"Right," I announce, lifting her up and off me in order to stop myself from saying 'fuck it' to interruptions, mentally calculating how long Brody might be happy talking away to himself.

I stand up, adjusting my insistent hard-on in the process before gently pushing her back down into the one-seater and returning her confiscated coffee mug.

"You finish your morning zombie routine, and I'll go sort the boy out." Her eyes go soft and her lips part and I know I just scored points with that.

"Okay," she replies with a content smile. "Bring me our boy."

18

Amy

I'm a nervous wreck by the time Saturday comes around because this afternoon, my son is going to meet his biological father.

I knew that Ryan would come back to Chicago at some point, but I was never sure whether he would want to see his son. He was not in a good place when he left last year and as much as Sean and Sam tried to help him, he didn't seem to want to help himself.

But after our phone conversation last week, I have a small sliver of hope that maybe he might want to step up to the plate where Brody is concerned.

That brings up a whole host of other issues though, like how Thomas feels about this whole situation.

As much as he has tried to assure me that he is okay with today's meeting, he's been distracted all week. But he has been with us whenever he's not working. He's slept in my bed every night this week and although I might be looking for problems where there aren't any, I swear he's been touching me more, holding me longer and squeezing me just a little bit tighter.

I am so thankful he's coming with us today. We're meeting Ryan at one o'clock at the children's zoo in Lincoln Park. It'll give us a good hour until Brody's due for his afternoon nap and therefore, not put too much pressure on anyone—especially Ryan—for this first meeting.

"Stop chewing your nails," Thomas says, walking out of the kitchen with Brody on his hip. "I like it when you dig them into my back and you won't be able to do that if you bite them all off."

Dropping my hand, I look up from the couch and meet his amused eyes, still loving the way he looks with my son.

"I don't know what's going to happen today. I *hate* not knowing what to expect."

Thomas crosses the room, setting Brody down on his blanket and handing him his favorite toy truck before sitting down and pulling me sideways into his lap. He wraps an arm around my waist and cups my jaw with his hand as I turn to face him.

"You do know I am capable of talking without being in your lap."

"I like you here," he says with a gentle squeeze. "Now tell me what's really going on."

"What if he doesn't like him?" I say quietly.

"It's impossible not to love Brody."

"I mean, what if Brody doesn't like Ryan."

His brow furrows and his body tenses beneath me. *That hit a nerve.*

"You're always going to have me, sweetness. I'm not going anywhere." *Wow, nothing gets past this guy does it?*

"I—" His fingers flex on my face.

"Amy, I'm here for you and I'm here for Brody. He may not be my blood but I love him as if he was, just as I love you unconditionally. We'll get through today, we'll get through tomorrow and everything else life decides to throw at us. Whatever happens, I am here."

I breathe out a huge sigh of relief. It's not that I didn't know how Thomas felt about us but right now, I really needed to hear that.

I dip my head and kiss him, starting out soft and slow, wanting to show him how grateful I am to have him in my life. But as always, the light lip touch morphs into something more —something deeper and harder—as the need to reassure myself takes over.

When we finally break apart, I rest my forehead against his as we breathe each other in and recover.

"We need to get going," he says roughly, his voice betraying just how affected he still is after our kiss.

"Yeah."

"I love you, sweetness. Always remember that. Okay?"

For words that should reassure me, so why does that unsettle me?

Thirty minutes later and we're standing at the entrance to the zoo when I see Ryan and Sean walking along the path toward us.

"Shit, shit, shit," I mutter under my breath. Thomas wraps his arm around my hips and gives my hip a gentle squeeze.

He turns his head so his mouth is by my ear, "It's going to be fine. Relax."

"I need a valium, or vodka . . . maybe both," I whisper, earning a chuckle from Thomas.

"I'll give you whatever you need when we get home."

"Well, that's something to look forward to at least," I murmur just as the men reach us. Sean looks at me with soft eyes—a rare and treasured occurrence—before shaking Thomas's hand and clapping him on the shoulder.

"Hey," I say to Ryan who's notably standing back from us. His eyes are glued on our son who's sitting up in the stroller, happily babbling away to his stuffed giraffe toy that Thomas bought him on our last trip to the zoo.

"Ry?" Sean says, narrowing his eyes as his brother stands stock-still, staring at Brody.

Ryan's eyes move up to me, and I'm shocked to see they're wet.

"Ahh . . . sorry," he says, swiping at his face. "I didn't expect him to be so big. You've done an amazing job, Amz." I don't know what it is, but I sag into Thomas's side at Ryan's words.

"Sweetness?" Thomas asks, pulling me into him.

I swallow down the lump in my throat and look up, his face full of concern. "We can—"

"No, I'm fine." I stand up straight and look at Ryan, smiling at him. "Should we go find somewhere to sit down? I know Brody would probably love to get out onto the grass." I point over to a clearing in the park.

"Yeah, sounds good," Ryan replies gruffly.

Once Thomas has pulled Brody out of the stroller, he hands

him to me and gives me a grin and a wink before moving over to the park bench and taking a seat beside Sean.

Sitting down cross-legged on the grass, I put Brody down, letting him lean against me. Ryan joins us but gives us space. He still seems incapable of tearing his eyes away from our son.

"I can't get over how he looks. He's like the perfect mix of you and me."

I hook a hand around Brody's tummy as he lurches forward, the blades of grass his chosen target.

"No, baby, you can't eat that." Of course he doesn't care what I say because he's almost seven months old and already has a mind of his own. I lift him up, holding him out to Ryan.

"I, um . . . shit," he says as he awkwardly places his hands around Brody's back and pulls him down to sit in his lap. Brody's face scrunches up and he balls his hands into tight little fists.

I scoot over and hold his hand, his body relaxing when he sees me there with him. Ryan's face totally gives him away, he's tense and unsure of what to do and Brody is picking up on it.

Turning my head, I look over to Thomas and Sean. The latter giving me a reassuring chin lift but I don't miss Thomas's expression before he tries to hide it from me. He smiles but it is half-hearted at best. His eyes are stuck on Brody sitting in Ryan's lap, and maybe me kneeling next to them too. His mouth is moving and he's nodding at whatever Sean is saying, but his squared shoulders and twitching jaw speaks volumes.

A wail from Brody grabs my attention and Ryan quickly hands him back to me. Brody looks over my shoulder and holds his arms out, wanting Thomas and grunting his disapproval when he can't reach him, something Ryan definitely doesn't miss.

"Are you happy?" he asks, shocking the shit out of me.

Cradling Brody against my shoulder, I rub his back and meet Ryan's eyes. "Yeah, I really am."

He opens his mouth to say something else but decides otherwise, closing it again. We sit there in silence, Ryan's arms crossed over his chest, his body language definitely of a man who's shutting down emotionally. It soon becomes obvious that I'm going to have to be the one to say what we're both thinking.

"Ryan, I know you're probably feeling guilty about leaving and I definitely know that this whole situation is probably a lot to take in right now."

"You got that right."

"But really," I say, reaching out and putting my hand on his arm. "I might've been hard at the start but I've got a lot of people in my life that have helped me."

"Thomas?"

"Especially him. But Sean and Sam too, my dad and stepmom, everyone."

"That's good, Amz, and I'm really glad that you have that. I just . . . I just don't see where I fit into all of this."

Brody starts to fuss again, wriggling against me and wanting to be anywhere but here.

"I'll take him," Thomas says from beside us, and never have I been more grateful for this man of mine than right now. I smile up at him as he grabs Brody from me. His mouth is tight and I can't read what he's thinking, and I can usually *always* read him.

Watching my boys walk away, I see Thomas's whole

demeanor change and he's grinning at my son, bouncing him in his arms and making Brody squeal with glee.

Turning back to Ryan, I see his eyes watching the scene play out in front of us too.

"I could never be like that, the way he is with him. It's just not me," he says and I can see the pain in his features. There's a lot of regret there.

"I may have been mad at the time, but if you'd never left, I wouldn't have the life I have now, and I wouldn't change that for the world."

"I have something I need to talk to you about. Do you think we could meet this week?"

Tilting my head, I study him for a moment. "You can tell me anything, Ryan. What's this abo—"

"Amz?" Thomas calls out to me.

Ryan moves toward the park bench where the guys are sitting and the amused look on Thomas and Sean's faces have me snorting like a pig as I grin at them.

"Brody decided to mark the occasion with a number three," Thomas announces, making Sean laugh. "There's no way we can clean him up here. We probably need to go back to the car because this load is going to take an army of supplies."

I shake my head and snicker. "Okay, well it looks like we're going then." I grab hold of the stroller and turn to Ryan. "I'm sorry, but my son—our son—has an amazing talent when it comes to filling his diaper."

Ryan scrunches his nose up. "Is that smell coming from him?" he asks, sounding horrified.

I laugh at him, just this comical moment showing me how far he's got to go to be ready for anything resembling an unsupervised visit.

"Do you think you could come over to Sean's place one day next week? We really need to talk about stuff," Ryan asks.

I scan his face, looking for any sign that I'm going to like this talk or not.

"I should be able to. I'll just need to check with Thomas and—"

"Can he watch Brody for you? So that we can talk?" *Jeez, he really wants this.*

"Should be fine but I'll text you tonight and let you know, okay?"

He sighs, his shoulders dropping in obvious relief.

"You guys all good?" Sean asks, sidling up to me and wrapping an arm around my shoulders. "Thomas has gone to deal with Brody's attempt at wiping out world disease, one poop at a time." *Shit. I didn't even realize he'd left.*

I look around to see Thomas and Brody twenty feet down the path in the direction of the parking lot. "Crap. I better go help him." I give Sean a squeeze and kiss his cheek before taking a step toward Ryan to do the same but suddenly stopping myself in an awkward mid-hug stance.

Ryan's lips twitch whereas his brother just straight out laughs. "Never change, Amz." Sean wraps his hand around my head and brushes his lips against my temple before moving away.

I flip them both off and wave to them over my shoulder as I run after Thomas letting Brody's stroller lead the way.

As far as the first-time meeting between my baby and the biological father, that was weird and at times I could tell Ryan was uncomfortable—okay, *way* out of his element—but I imagine most newbie parents are like that, especially when they have no experience with babies.

Overall though, I don't think it was a complete disaster, as long as you forget that I was wound so tight it's a wonder I didn't bust a nut or something. And let's not forget that Brody —although normally the easiest baby in the world—didn't seem to want anything to do with Ryan, instead wanting Mommy or Thomas.

Other than that, I think today went well.

I catch up to my boys just as they reach Thomas's SUV.

"Hey, want some help?" I say snaking my arms around his waist from behind.

He looks over his shoulder and grins at me. "I'm game if you are . . ." He hands over my very smelly and adorably-happy-about-it son and shakes his head, his lips curling up in what could only be a mix of disgust and amusement. "But next time, let's bring gas masks."

With the light in his eyes and the smirk on his face, the tight coil in my stomach eases and all is right in the world again.

Now I've just got to get through whatever Ryan wants to talk to me about and life will be peachy.

19

Thomas

It shouldn't bother me.

I've never been the type of man to feel insecure or even unsure of himself in any situation—getting chlamydia notwithstanding of course.

But something about Ryan turning back up on the scene has unsettled me.

I can admit it now. Seeing him holding Brody in his arms felt wrong. It shouldn't get to me so much. I shouldn't *let* it get to me so much. I spent the whole time stiff as a board, something that Sean did not miss.

"You've got nothing to worry about, Thomas. I promise you."

Tearing my eyes away—more for my sanity than anything else—I turned toward my friend.

"I really want to believe you here and I'm sorry if this offends you, but from what I remember of your brother, he's not exactly Mr. reliable and responsible. Case in point, the fact he walked away from Amy when she got pregnant."

Sean's eyes didn't go hard as expected. Instead, they softened with understanding. "I get you," he said quietly, his gaze returning to where Brody was fussing in Sean's brother's lap. "And I sincerely hope he does stay sober this time. But I've got almost twenty years experience that tells me otherwise. He has his head screwed on straight when it comes to this though. You have my word on that, Thomas."

"Doesn't make it any easier seeing the boy I think of as my son being introduced to his father."

"You're more of a father to Brody than Ryan is and ever will be, Thomas," he says without hesitation. "I've watched you from before he was even born and you may not have seen your life leading you to where you are now, but not once have I seen you hesitate when it comes to stepping up for Amy or your son."

Hearing him say that—a man who I have so much respect for—makes my heart swell with pride. Not only at myself, but for the family that Amy and I have made. A family that I would do anything for.

One of the hardest things to do in the park was sit there and not go to Brody when he started fussing and wanting either Amy or myself to pick him up. He was obviously picking up on Ryan's nerves but there was nothing I could've done—or should've done—to help. It wasn't my place to step in, Brody seemed confused enough as it was.

But when I saw him wanting to get down when Amy and Ryan were having what looked like a serious conversation, I decided it was time to step in.

Then my boy proceeded to decimate his diaper—and then some—so our park visit came to a premature end.

During the drive home, Amy tells me everything Ryan

said, including his request for a meeting with Sean next weekend. I have no idea what he wants to discuss with her, but I trust Sean implicitly, so I'm not worried about that small detail. Honestly, I think it's smart for Ryan and Amy to discuss how things might work moving forward.

Having survived diaper-geddon, Amy takes Brody into his room for a nap when we get to her apartment, leaving me to grab a beer from the fridge and relax in the living room.

I'm trying to be a good guy here, I *want* Brody to know his real father and hopefully have a relationship with him in the future. But where does that leave me? Will it confuse him if I'm around when Ryan's around? Will I have to make myself scarce whenever Ryan comes to visit?

How can I make this easier for them all without losing everyone I love?

"Stop that." Amy's voice is a hissed whisper, cutting the air like a knife. My wide eyes snap up to find her standing a few feet away from me, hands on her hips and an expression that could only be described as murderous.

She closes the distance between us and I swear I can feel the anger radiating off her. "You know that habit I have of saying my thoughts out loud?" And I realize then just *why* she's so annoyed.

"Yeah, and I'm telling you now to get those ideas out of your head right now, Thomas John Caldwell." She leans down so her finger is poking my chest and her face is in mine. "You are *not* going to be the good guy, the nice guy, the one who's going to step aside so that Brody can have a relationship with his biological father just because you have some preconceived notion that he needs to have that." *Whoa, she really can read minds.*

"Sweetness, I was just—"

She straddles my lap and I juggle the beer bottle down to the floor before resting my hands on her hips, not willing to take my chances with wrapping my arms around her when she's on a tear like this.

"You do not get to even *consider* walking away from us now."

"I wasn't—"

"You said to me 'Anything you need, anytime you need it' just yesterday." She drops her voice low to mimic me and needing to break the awkward tension between us, I can't help the snicker that escapes my lips.

She shakes my shoulders. "Don't try and charm me now, I'm pissed."

"I see that." My lips twitch and I struggle to control myself.

She huffs and growls under her breath. "Of course I'd end up with a sexy handsome man who could grin his way out of a paper bag without even batting an eyelid."

I quirk a brow, my mouth curved up in a full-on grin now, all previous melancholy completely disappeared. "A paper bag? Really?"

"Thomas . . ." she sighs, leaning her head close to mine. "Tell me how you're really feeling about all of this because I need to know whether you are okay with Ryan being in Brody's life, if that's what he wants to do."

I don't hesitate with my response. "Are *you* okay with it?" I don't have to think about it because seeing Ryan with his son today, with their matching eyes and hair, I think Ryan deserves at least one chance—and only one—to do right by his son.

"Well, I'm not fully on 'Team Responsible Ryan.' There's

a lot of ground to make up there." She leans back a little but her eyes stay with me.

"I could give you guys some space. You know, give Brody time to get used to Ryan being around?" My voice vibrates with uncertainty. Could I actually walk away—albeit temporarily—to give Ryan and Brody a chance to bond? I would if that's what was necessary, doesn't mean I wouldn't rip myself apart while waiting to come back though.

"How about this?" she says, her tone sharp and to the point. "We're used to having *you* around, and now you're saying you'd be willing to leave us?"

"This is not me ending things. It would be stepping aside to give Ryan a chance at being a dad to his son, giving Brody the chance to get to know his father. I'd do it if that's what you and Ryan wanted."

"Fuck that," she spits out angrily. "I love my son to the moon and back and would do anything and everything for him, but *you* are his dad, Thomas. *You* are the one who has been there for his whole life, even when you didn't have to, before this wonderful, amazing, best-thing-in-the-world thing happened between the two of us, you had a relationship with Brody." Her voice drops to a shaky whisper. "I don't want you to ever think that Ryan could replace you. He can't and he won't. You have to believe that."

I run my hands up her side until my fingers frame the soft skin of her neck. "I want to do right by you guys."

"Then don't leave us, don't give us space, don't change a goddamn thing," she says on a whispered shout. "Being a sperm donor does not make a father, you are living proof of that. Your dad another perfect example. Brody loves *you*. I love *you*. You're the one who's been here since his first breath and he'll be with us when it comes time for us to take our last."

My eyes soften and my body sags back into the couch. "You always know the right thing to say, sweetness."

"It's part of my charm," she says with a shrug.

"You're also cute when you're feisty. This doesn't bode well for my future."

She narrows her eyes at me—like she does every time I call her cute—but shakes her head and presses her chest into mine, tipping her head back in the process, an offer I don't turn down as I brush my lips against hers. "I need to know you're doing okay, Thomas. Whatever else happens now or in the future, you and Brody are my priorities. Everything else comes after that."

He pulls his head back, his eyes boring into mine as they roam over my face. "You totally mean that don't you. I thought *I* was the one that's meant to reassure *you*."

"It's the new millennium. Women can do everything men can do, even pee standing up if we want, so if I need to step up and make sure you know just how much you're wanted and needed in this little family of ours, you can be damn well sure I'm gonna do it."

20

Amy

The past week has flown by and now it's Saturday, 'Meeting with Ryan' day.

I leave Brody with Thomas at his apartment, having put Brody down for his afternoon sleep in the Pack 'n Play in the guest room.

"It'll be fine," Thomas says against my lips, pressing me into the wall beside his front door and kissing me breathless.

"You're not making it easy to leave."

"I'm not trying to. I'm just making sure you're coming back to me." He runs kisses down my neck, driving me crazy and blowing my intentions to leave right out the window.

"You've got nothing to worry about there."

"Good," he whispers against my lips. "Now go so you can get back to your boys."

My boys. God, I love the sound of that more and more every time he says it.

Thirty minutes later, I drive up to the curb outside Sean and

Sam's house and turn off the engine. I take a moment to breathe, not sure what exactly Ryan wanted to talk about but feeling somewhat better knowing that Sean will be there. That's the only reason why Thomas agreed not to come. Not because he doesn't trust Ryan—although I think that is a contributing factor—but more the fact that he wanted to be here for me.

Breathing and surprisingly rational thinking completed, I step out of my car and walk along the path toward the house.

After Sean lets me in, a genuine smile on his face, I find Ryan sitting at the dining room table with a glass of orange juice in his hand. He scrapes his chair against the floor and stands up, walking toward me and giving me another awkward hug, but adding a kiss on the cheek to this one. *Okay, this is just weird now.*

"Okay, guys. You're kind of freaking me out here." I look between the both of them, not seeing any sign of stress or tension.

"Take a seat, Amz. Do you want a drink?"

I sit down and clasp my hands in front of me on the table and meet Ryan's eyes. "Please, Ryan. I just want to know what this is about. It's been nagging at me all week."

"All right," he says, scraping his hand through his hair and sitting down opposite me. Sean joins us, taking a seat at the end of the table.

Ryan clears his throat, his hands fidgeting with two yellow envelopes lying on the table in front of him.

"I . . ." he glances toward his brother who dips his chin in response. Ryan looks back at me, his shoulders rising and falling as he takes a slow deep breath.

"I've been sober for ninety days now but every day is still a struggle."

"That's good though, Ryan."

"It is." He nods, his fingers tracing the outline of the envelope.

"And it was good to meet Brody last weekend. He's a great kid."

"He is," I say with a smile, something that always happens when it comes to my son.

"But . . ."

"Ryan, please . . ." I beg. "Whatever it is, it'll be okay. Please just tell me what you wanted to talk about. If it's visitation rights or something like that, I'm open to talking about it. Thomas and I talked and—"

His eyes bore into me, a shine of unspoken emotion reflecting back at me.

"I met with a lawyer this week." My chest tightens, all the breath in my lungs catching in my throat, as I try to anticipate what his next sentence will be. "And I've had some papers drawn up." He places his palm on the left-most envelope and slides it across the table to me.

"Ryan, I wanted to talk to you so that we could—"

"Open it, Amz," Sean says quietly, his low voice echoing off the walls of the otherwise quiet house.

I ease the tab of the envelope open and reach inside, sliding out two pieces of paper.

Holding them up to read the first one, I quickly glance over at Ryan who's watching me closely, his hands clenched together in front of him. "The first one," he says, nodding to the papers in my hand, "is details of a trust that is set up for

Brody's education. Sean is the executor and will look after everything."

"Ryan, I—"

"Before you think I've done some big noble thing, let me explain. Our parents' estate allocated money for any children that Sean and I might have. Sean's kids each have this same trust and I wanted Brody to have the same. It's his right and he should have it."

I look at Sean who nods in agreement, showing me in that one movement that Ryan's telling the truth.

"I don't know what to say."

"Say thank you," Sean says, his lips curling up into a knowing half-grin. Looking back at Ryan, I see his shoulders loosen as he relaxes back into his chair. "Thank you, Ryan. This will help him do whatever he wants to do."

"It's not my money, Amz. This is something Brody is entitled to and I wanted to make sure he got it, whatever happens." Those words give me pause. *What does that mean?*

"Ryan." My voice is gentle, barely a whisper as I finally work it out. "You're leaving again, aren't you?"

He sits up straight and scrubs his face. "I've talked to my counselor. I've talked to my sponsor, and I've talked to Sam and Sean." Taking a deep breath, he leans his forearms on the table. "I'm not in a place to be the kind of person Brody needs or deserves in his life and I'm not sure I ever will be."

My heart aches for the man in front of me I once called a friend. Unable to stop myself, I put the papers on the table and get up from my seat, rounding the table and moving into the chair beside Ryan. He doesn't turn to face me though, the tick in his jaw working overtime as he struggles to keep his composure.

I reach out and cup his shoulder, finally getting his head to turn. My eyes sting as tears start to gather and fall. I know I should keep it together so that I can get Ryan through this but this side of him—the rarely seen selfless one—shows just how far he's come in his recovery.

"If Brody ever wants to know me—or anything about me—I'm not closing that door to him, but everything Sean's told me, everything I saw yesterday, I'm never going to be the father that Brody needs and honestly, he has everything he'll ever need from you and Thomas. He's Brody's father. I didn't make the best decision last year, but I'm sure as shit making the right one now. That notarized statement says I'm fully supportive of an application to terminate my parental rights in the event you would like Thomas to adopt Brody."

"Oh my God," I say, diving forward and wrapping my arms around Ryan's neck. Burying my face in his tee, barely restrained sobs—okay, I've got no control over them whatsoever—wrack through me and Ryan's arms soon come around me, no doubt to try and calm me down. Either that or he thinks some demon is trying to exorcise itself from my body.

"Are you sure? I would've never asked this of you," I whisper, wanting this to be for his ears only. I love Sean to death but I need to know that this is one hundred percent Ryan's decision. Sean would take a bullet for me, and would even go so far as to get his brother to walk away—again—if it was in Brody's best interests.

"That's why I'm giving it to you, to the three of you. What you do with that affidavit is up to you."

With wet eyes and a no-doubt blotchy face, I pull back and lightly punch him in the shoulder, his body jerking back slightly with the hit.

"What was that for?" he asks with a laugh.

"That's for making it impossible to hate you."

Thomas

"Da . . ."

"What buddy?"

"Da . . ."

"Ah okay. What do you want?" I ask and he leans forward, he pokes his clenched fist into my chest.

"Da . . . Da . . ." Holy shit. I freeze in place, not believing my ears but if the tightness in my chest is anything to go by, I didn't mishear.

I pull him into my lap, tilting my chin down and meeting a gummy grin.

"Buddy," I say gruffly, my throat thick with emotion.

It's one thing to give yourself to a woman and accept her child as your own. It's another for that child—almost seven-months-old—to acknowledge the bond in his own way, and Brody just did it in a sucker punch to the gut, shot to the heart, knock some sense into me kind of way like a Bon Jovi song on hyper drive.

Obviously in the moment, he reaches up and grips my lip with three fingers, pulling down hard enough to make my eyes water for an entirely different reason. I wrestle myself free but hold him up so we're face to face. "Love you too."

"Da." This time he dives at my face, giving me an open mouthed, drooly kiss.

A key in the lock grabs our attention and look over to see a beaming Amy walk into the apartment with a yellow envelope in her hand. I check my watch and see it's been over three hours since she was meant to meet Ryan.

I lift Brody into my arms and get off the floor, reaching her just in time for the baby to dive her way.

"Hey, baby. Did you miss me?" Brody gives Amy the same open mouth treatment which she laughs off as she pulls him into her chest. "Do I get the same treatment from my other favorite boy?" she asks, her eyes dancing as she looks over at me.

"Only if mine can be just as dribbly and wet."

"How do you make something so gross sound kinda dirty?"

"It's a talent." I close the distance between us and wrap my arm around her waist, pulling them both into me. She tips her face up just as I dip mine down, touching my lips to hers in a soft kiss that turns momentarily heated before easing back.

"Let me put him down and then we'll talk." She looks deeply into my eyes and I don't miss the weight of those words.

Something's happened, something *big*.

She takes Brody back over to the rug and sets him in the middle of his mountain of toys I'd constructed earlier, earning a squeal of delight before she takes a seat on the sofa, patting the cushion beside her.

I feel like I'm treading water and the *Jaws* soundtrack has just come on in surround sound. All I can do is remember what Amy and I promised each other.

We'll get through today, we'll get through tomorrow and everything else life decides to throw at us.

"Sweetness, please put me out of my misery. I've been fighting the urge to drive over to Sean's for the past few hours." She reaches over and grabs my hand, covering it with both of her own.

"Jesus, Amz, give me something to go on here. Was it bad? Does he want visitation or something?" Her eyes soften and her top teeth dig into her bottom lip as her gaze drops from my face and her thumb stroking my skin.

Taking a deep breath she squares her shoulders and looks up at me.

"Am I your last?" *What the fuck could've happened in the past two hours to have her questioning that?*

"You damn well know you are," I growl.

"And are you mine?"

"Always and forever if you'll have me," I say without hesitation. Never have I known something to be as true as that statement.

"Is Brody yours too?" My head jerks back, my chest tightening like a vise. If ever there was a moment in my life when I thought I might be having a heart attack, it would in this moment.

"In every possible way he can be." Her eyes are soft and shining with emotion. "What's going on? You're starting to scare me here. Did something happen with Ryan?"

"You could say that . . ."

"You're killing me here, Amz."

She moves one of her hands and reaches behind her back, her arm jostling around before resting her closed fist on her bouncing leg.

"Okay, I'm not a patient man when it comes to you, sweetness." Meeting my eyes, she watches me as she slides off the couch to kneel on the floor in front of me, turning her hand over and opening her fingers then the white box in her palm to reveal a wide platinum band.

Nope, that wasn't a heart attack before but I'm definitely having one now. I open my mouth to tell Amy there's a defibrillator in the lobby but nothing comes out, my jaw going slack as I sit there looking like a fish out of water.

For a man whose reputation is for always knowing what's going on and anticipating what comes next, the woman in front of me has completely blindsided me.

"Ryan gave me that today," she nods to the yellow envelope sitting on the couch, "and inside is the most selfless thing he could have ever done, a sworn statement supporting the termination of his parental rights." My breath catches and I freeze in place. *Never saw that coming.*

Her shoulders rise and she closes her eyes for a second, her lips moving in a silent whisper before she looks straight up at me, a new steely resolve in place. I look for any sign of sadness in her eyes but I see nothing but determination and certainty in her expression.

Reaching forward, I cradle her outstretched hand and give her fingers a gentle squeeze.

"I love you, Thomas John Caldwell," she says, her voice rough as her body trembles, her bottom lip quivering as she forges on. "I cannot imagine Brody growing up without you in his life to love him and guide him toward being the best man he could be. And I know there's nobody else in the world who could do that because you're the best man I know."

"Sweetness," I barely get the word out, my throat has a lump the size of Lake Michigan blocking it.

Amy tilts her head and with shaking fingers, deftly removes the ring and places the box on the floor before grabbing hold of my hand and sliding the ring onto the ring finger of my left hand.

"Be my last just as I am yours." She seats the ring against my knuckle and dips her head to kiss it.

"Fuck, Amy. Yes."

Her eyes widen when I drop to my knees on the floor, matching her stance.

"Yes?" she asks, her eyes wide and wondrous.

"Fuck yes," I counter with a grin.

"Anything with the word yes in it sounds good to me."

I wrap my arms around her waist and jerk her body against mine, thighs to chest, her arms forced to grab hold of my shoulders. Touching my forehead to hers, our lips a whisper's breath apart, I take in the woman who just asked to spend forever with me.

I close the half-inch between us to kiss her but her fingers on my shoulders tense and hold me back. Lifting my head back I quirk an eyebrow at her, puzzled even more when I see a beaming smile on her face.

"I have one more life-changing question for you."

"The answer is yes, it's always yes for you, don't you know that by now?"

Her whole expression goes melty and it just makes me want to kiss her more than I did before, which was a hell of a lot.

"I want you to adopt my son. Will you be Brody's dad?" Nope, *this* is a heart attack. Actually, a heart *explosion*.

Amy runs her hands up my neck until her forearms are resting on my chest and her fingers are cupping my jaw.

"Abso-fucking-lutely." Then I've had enough. I run my hand up her back, tangling my fingers in her hair and I kiss her, starting hard and with purpose, morphing into slow and meaningful, pouring everything I'm feeling and everything I am into it.

That's until I feel a tugging on my pants from the floor beside me. We pull apart and both look down to be met by the toothless smile of Brody.

Our son.

But wait…

EPILOGUE

EIGHTEEN MONTHS & ONE WEDDING LATER

Amy

As is the way with our now very large group of friends, whenever there's a birth, death, marriage, new job, old job, holiday, start—and end—of a season, anything we can celebrate, we do it.

So really it's no surprise that it's a Saturday afternoon and all of us are gathered in the backyard of my new house with Thomas and Brody. We had been living in my apartment until last weekend when we finally moved into our new five bedroom, three bathroom dream home in the same neighborhood as Noah and Zoe. It's family friendly, close to great schools and although we took our time to find our forever home, I'm so glad we waited to get it just right.

I still work for Sean, but now I run all of the administration and accounts for his three bars and clubs, not just Throb. To make it even better, I work from home three days a week so that I can spend as much time as I can with Brody. The other two days a week when I have to travel into the city, it's Thomas who has our son home with him.

Yes, our son. Thomas legally adopted Brody shortly after our wedding.

But today is a big day in Chez Caldwell. We're welcoming all of our friends into our home to celebrate the start of an amazing new life for us.

With the gaggle of kids playing on our back lawn, all of us women decided early on that it was probably best that we stayed close in case of child emergencies e.g. fights, spills, accidents and the like.

Sitting around the brand spanking new outdoor table with the rest of the girls, I spot Thomas walking out of the kitchen's French doors and heading our way just as Kate and Zander's seven-year-old daughter Rose comes walking up to her mother.

"Mommy?" Rose asks, standing next to Kate and tugging on her top.

Kate takes a sip of wine before looking down at her daughter with a smile on her face. "Yeah, princess?"

"What's an ortasm?"

Wine shoots out of Kate's mouth and she starts choking. The rest of us either gasp, snort, or in Mac's case, cackle with laughter.

Noah and Zoe's Nate, never one to miss out on being the center of attention, decides to wade in with his five-year-old wisdom.

"I have a penith," he says before proceeding to pull down his pants and prove the fact.

"Oh God, I can't breathe," Abi wheezes, bent over in her chair and laughing like a loon.

"Daddy says that he'll cut off any boy's penis that touches me," Sean and Sam's gorgeous eight-year-old daughter Megan informs the group.

"He'd be right, pumpkin," Sam replies, pursing her lips and not looking at all surprised by her daughter's announcement.

"I'm so glad Riley can't hear us. You don't want to know the things she comes out with," Mac adds, looking over her shoulder to where her now ten-year-old daughter was playing a few minutes ago. "Shit," she mutters when Riley appears right beside her.

"Daddy told me I'm not allowed to talk about penises. But if you can then I can."

"Riley, this is an adult conversation. Remember we talked about that?"

"But I found a huge plastic penis in that red box at the back of your closet and *you* told me it was a paper weight." Mac's faces goes red and her lips twitch.

"Ah . . . yeah honey, it is."

"That's good because I put it on Daddy's desk in his office. You shouldn't hide things like that."

The rest of the group struggle to stifle their laughter but somehow Mac powers through it. "Why were you in my closet, missy?"

Riley shrugs, her hand darting out to grab a handful of potato chips from the bowl in the middle of the table. "I was looking for the chicken."

We all go silent, waiting for the penny to drop.

Mac's head jerks back. "What?"

"Oh no, I'm not sure I *want* to know where this is going . . ." Abi says quietly beside us.

"I heard you say you wanted Daddy's cock." Riley turns to her mother and narrows her eyes, her hands moving to her hips as she takes a hilarious—and very indignant—pose. "You shouldn't hide Daddy's cock. It's mean for Daddy to keep a chicken inside."

"Ah . . ." Mac's wide eyes move to Kate.

"Riley," Kate says, her voice full of humor. "I think you should go ask your daddy about his chicken. Make sure you do it so that all of the uncles can hear too. I bet they'll love to hear about the chicken."

"I think I will," she states with a firm nod before turning on her heels and leaving the room in search of her father.

"I swear to God that child is not mine," Mac says with a laugh.

"Oh, no. She's totally you. Head to toe," Thomas adds, a huge grin on his face that just gets bigger when Mac pokes her tongue out at him.

"Baby?" I ask, bending my head back to look up at my husband. His eyes go soft in that way I love and part of me wants to jump him then and there.

"Yes, sweetness." He dips his head down, resting his hands on the arms of my chair and bringing his mouth close to mine.

"Do you want to get everyone outside? I've got a few things I want to say." I reach up and run my fingers through the short stubble on his cheeks and jaw. I was never a huge facial hair fan until he got past the rough and scratchy phase of beard growth. Now it's at the soft and tickly stage, let's just say I'm a big advocate. Some might even say huge.

Beards for the win, I say. Or at least, I always win when that beard is close to certain body parts.

Wanting a kiss, I pull his lips to mine and ease my tongue into his mouth, his answering groan everything I need in my life.

"You play dirty."

"I play to win, like every good woman should. If that means dirty, then so be it."

"And you do it well, wife. Give me a minute and I'll have everyone out here. Cameron just arrived too."

I jerk my head back, surprised that Cade's twin brother Cameron finally accepted an invitation to a group gathering. Cade's sister Callie, her husband, Jonathan, and their two kids are permanent fixtures at our get-togethers but Cam has been a bit reclusive since he got out of the army eighteen months ago.

Something tells me that Cam is going to have his own dose of drama soon. At least this time, it won't be me having to hold on for dear life while experiencing it firsthand.

As promised, Thomas returns a few moments later with Brody in his arms and the rest of our guests trailing behind him. I stand up and move around the crowd to stand facing everyone, looking toward my partner in crime and giving her a nod.

Daniel walks over to Mac, his lips twitching as he reaches her side. "I hear we have a chicken problem at home."

Abi and I snicker as we walk past them, not helped by Mac's audible snort as she bursts out laughing and buries her face in Daniel's neck.

Mia and Zoe also stand, lifting their two chairs and carrying them to their pre-planned place opposite me but at the front of the group before taking their place next to their respective husbands.

"Brody, come to Mommy," I say, crouching down and waiting while a confused Thomas lets our son down to the ground. When Brody reaches me he claps excitedly and wraps his arms around my shoulders, holding on for dear life as I stand up straight, taking him with me just as Abi reaches my side.

"You ready for this?" she whispers under her breath.

"Are you?"

"Abso-fuck—I mean, fudging-lutely."

"Thomas and Cade, we need you to take a seat right here," I announce, pointing our two very confused—if their furrowed brows are anything to go by—and out-of-the-know husbands to the two chairs in front of us.

The rest of our friends gather behind the guys, forming a natural semi-circle.

Taking a deep breath, I turn to Abi and her glassy eyes and struggle to swallow down the huge lump in my throat.

I lean in so my mouth is by her ear while trying to contain a squirming Brody desperately trying to attach himself to his Aunty Abi. "You ready for this?"

"Yeah."

"So," I say, facing back to the group and a wary-looking Thomas who's watching me like a hawk. I reach down and grab Abi's hand, giving her fingers a squeeze and grinning. "Abi, Brody, and I would like to make an announcement."

"We're kinda getting that impression," Zander calls out from behind Thomas.

"I know we talked about swinging, Spitfire, but I didn't think you'd want to tell the world about it," Cade says with a shit-eating smirk. Somehow I don't think he's going to be laughing in a few minutes.

"Amy and I are running off together." And the air goes completely still.

I decide to take it a step further, wrapping my arm around Abi's waist and pulling her into my side. "We're in love and we can't deny it any longer." I struggle to get out the words, switching from Thomas's amused eyes to Cade's narrowed ones before dissolving into giggles.

Thankfully Abi is able to maintain at least a little composure. "Come here Brody, you have to give Daddy and Uncle Cade their presents now." My son claps and scrambles out of my arms, launching himself into his godmother's arms.

Abi crouches down, letting him stand on the ground before handing him two white boxes from a paper bag behind her.

"So you're not leaving them then?" Matt says. "I thought for sure you'd finally come to your senses and were ready to join my harem."

I shoot him a grin. "You barely handle Mia, let alone the two of us."

"Amen to *that,* sister," Mia replies with a laugh.

With the presents in hand, Brody walks over to Thomas first, throwing the box at him rather than handing it over before running—yes actually *running*—to Cade and jumping in his lap.

"Now you're taking my son and your wife is taking *my* wife?" Thomas says, his lips twitching.

"Seems like it. Should we hook up too? I mean, I've already seen you naked so—"

"Is it just me, or has this night suddenly turned into a scene out of the Twilight Zone?" Mac says with a shake of her head.

"When it comes to you, *nothing* is too farfetched. What makes you think our friends would be any different?" Daniel says. "I mean, you told our daughter a sex toy was a paper weight, nothing could beat *that.*"

"Can I open it?" Thomas asks, bringing everyone's attention back to us and the white box he's holding.

"Wait!" Abi shrieks. "You both have to open them together."

Cade and Thomas look at each other with matching 'what the fuck' expressions before returning their eyes to their respective wives.

"Okay, go."

"Go, Daddy, go!" Brody squeals, bouncing excitedly in Cade's lap.

"Right, buddy. Want to help me?" Thomas barely gets the words out before our son catapults himself sideways, replacing Cade's lap with his father's one.

Balancing Brody on one leg, Thomas meets my eyes, his face turning soft and sexy, a playful smile playing at his lips.

"Go on, Daddy," I rasp, my throat tight because of that damn lump in it. I blink rapidly, trying to hold back the inevitable tears that are going to strike at any moment.

Thomas—with Brody's help—slowly opens the lid of the box, his eyes narrowing on the black tissue paper inside.

"You too, Cade," Abi says, walking over to where he's sitting. Kneeling on the ground in front of him, she rests her hands on his knees, eagerly waiting for his reaction to what's in the box.

Everyone watches the scene play out, the girls leaning forward to see what the deal is.

Thomas is the first to pull back the wrapping, pulling out a white piece of card and reading it. I see his face turn from intrigued to awe, his wide eyes snapping up to mine.

"Sweetness," he says in the roughest voice I've ever heard from him. He stands, hooking Brody on his hip and carrying both our son and the box toward me.

I don't need to look over at Cade and Abi to know what

he's unveiled; a bread roll with a card that simply says Bun in the Oven. And since Cade and Abi have been trying for so long to get pregnant, I know that this moment is extra special for them.

The card that moved my husband so much that he had to be near me said "The only thing better than having you as a husband, is having you as the father of our children . . ." What he didn't pull out of the box was the white cotton onesie that says 'Hey Dad, See you soon.'

As soon as I'm within reach, Thomas wraps his hand around the back of my neck and leans forward to touch his forehead to mine. "We're having a baby," he whispers and looking deep into his eyes, I can see they're wet.

Only two times have I seen Thomas show so much emotion; the day he delivered Brody on that grocery store floor, and the day we got married on the shore of Lake Michigan.

Putting my arms around both of my boys, I tilt my chin and gently kiss my husband, pouring everything into that one lip touch, knowing just how much we both want this baby, this family, this life.

"Get a room," Mia teases, breaking me out of the moment. Thomas and I turn to the group of our friends and loved ones, my eyes first seeking out my beaming father and crying stepmother, before running over a grinning Mia, a smiling Kate, a soft-eyed Sam—which is a miracle in itself—a making-out-with-her-husband Dani, a laughing Zoe, and a bemused Mac.

I finally stop on Sean. The man who's been like a big brother to me, who has always been there for anything I've ever needed. For an intense guy, he's actually a big softie when you find that sweet spot.

He doesn't smile at us, but he meets my eyes and nods, knowing that no words are needed because there's nothing left to say.

I have my son, I have the love of my perfect husband, and I'm carrying a second child we've been so desperately waiting for.

I have my happy forever after and finally—*finally*—a lifetime of big whooshes that I know will never end.

Everything I ever wanted. Everything Thomas gave to me.

Thomas

When looking back at the past few years—having been graced with everything I've ever wanted—I find myself reflecting on what led me to this point in my life.

The conclusion I've come to is simple.

Life is a series of decisions and consequences. They can be good, they can be bad, they can be dangerous, and occasionally surprising. And then sometimes, you get an STD, make a vow of chastity, and it leads you to a woman and son that make your life feel complete.

And as weird as it sounds, there's not one thing I would change about my past. It led me to this moment in time. The love of a good woman, a son that may not be my blood, but is mine in every other way, a house, the figurative white picket fence, and—finally—my very own happy ending. So shout out to the girl who gave me the Clam, it may not have been fun at the time but it's worth everything now.

The game is now done, the end is here, and lucky me, I've won the best prize of them all.

So thank you chlamydia, you stung, you burned, you were a total pain in the ass, but without you, I wouldn't be where I am right now; a wife, a mine in every way possible son, and another much wanted child.

A full and happy life.

And I wouldn't have it any other way.

The next book in the series is Promising Bliss - Cam and Sarah's story. Keep reading for a sneak peek.

PROMISING BLISS SNEAK PEEK

Sarah

I swipe an eye shadow brush over my eyelid, blink at the wrong time, and end up trying to pretty my eyeball instead of the skin above it.

Deep breath in. Deep breath out.

Remember what Mom always says: "Everything happens for a reason."

Dropping the brush into the sink, I snatch a wash cloth from the bathroom counter and scrub my eye like my sight depends on it—which it probably does.

I try positive visualization to calm my nerves: a hot beach, a fruity cocktail, soft white sand beneath me, crystal blue water for miles, and the gorgeous man I used to love lying next to me.

Shaking my head, I drop my chin and try the breathing thing again. *What am I thinking?*

I tossed and turned all night, dozing off at dawn only to sleep through my alarm. And when I finally did wake up, it was in a cold sweat, having dreamed of a life full of regret if I followed through with today's two o'clock appointment.

Am I about to make the biggest mistake of my life? I always figured I'd get married, just not to my best friend and for money, nonetheless.

I have no other choice that I can see. It's my last resort after exhausting all other possibilities.

My soon-to-be spouse—my best friend, Wyatt—would never do me wrong, and is stepping up to help by becoming my husband. Together, our combined income will allow me to borrow enough to cover my parents' overdue property taxes.

Dad lost his job last year when the big finance firm he had been working for since I was a kid slashed hundreds of jobs after a scandal involving the CEO. With Mom in and out of hospital with Lupus, neither of them were bringing in any money. They lived off Dad's severance package for a few months but then started to struggle. What I didn't realize until a month ago was just *how* bad things had gotten. When I found out that a lien had been put on the property by a tax buyer and a huge sum of money was needed for my parents to clear their house title and be able to sell their place, I felt compelled to do something.

As soon as I found out, I went online and applied for any and every loan available. When that failed, I met with my bank manager, then my boss, trying to find a way to raise the money I would need to save the house.

I even tried to sell my car, hoping that any payment to the government would be better than *no* payment. My father put a stop to that particular option almost immediately, telling me in no uncertain terms that I either stopped what I was doing or else he'd lock me in my cotton candy pink bedroom to teach me a lesson. When I retorted that he wouldn't be able to do that if he didn't have the house, he muttered some rather unmentionable words under his breath and walked away.

It was the truth though, and both Mom and Dad knew it.

Last weekend, when it appeared that all hope was lost, I drowned my sorrows with copious amounts of gin and tonic. When Wyatt came home from his hospital shift where he works as a pediatric nurse, he found me white girl wasted on the couch with a bowl of potato chips in one hand and tissues in the other while I sobbed over *Bride Wars*.

But being the amazing human being that he is, Wyatt sat down, pulled me into his lap and cuddled me while we watched the prince find his princess. Then he made me a strong coffee, effectively poured it down my throat, and asked me to spill the beans.

So I did. I told him everything.

That was when he shocked the shit out of me and asked me to marry him.

When I asked what his *boyfriend* Mark might think about it, he shrugged, and said, "Sez, if I'm going to marry a woman, you're the only one I want it to be."

Of course at the time, I was totally on board the wedding train. The next morning I had a little trepidation but knew it was a good compromise because together, our combined income would definitely qualify us for a big enough loan, and I could help my parents out and save the house.

But when I woke up this morning, a seemingly normal wedding-day Wednesday, there was a deep ache in my chest, the likes of which I hadn't felt for years.

Opening my eyes, I stare at myself in the mirror and catch the reflection of my alarm clock in my bedroom.

"Shit!" I shriek, clutching the towel wrapped around me as I run into my bedroom, grab the black garment bag from inside my closet door, and carefully lay it on my bed before throwing my towel to the side.

It's then I glance up and meet the very wide eyes of my teenage boy neighbor across the street whose living room window looks straight through my *open* curtains.

He stands there frozen with a huge goofy grin on his face while I scream bloody murder and scramble to find my towel, slipping on a wayward sock and kicking my nightstand in the process, bending my little toe the wrong way.

Now I'm naked, jumping on the spot like a kangaroo with my leg bent as I hold my foot, trying to ease the pain. Giving up on regaining any dignity, I drop to the floor and crawl around my bed to my window, jerking my curtains shut before collapsing front first on the floor.

Not going to be able to look that guy in the eyes again, that's for sure.

My cell phone rings from the bathroom, and with a defeated sigh, I hoist myself up off the floor to go fetch it.

"Hey Wyatt," I say, struggling to catch my breath.

"Sez, you okay?"

"Yeah. Why wouldn't I be?" I'm lying through my teeth here.

"You were kind of weird last night, more than normal, so I wanted to check in. Are you on your way?"

"No," I reply with a huff. "I woke up late after *barely* sleeping, then flashed the neighbor's son, and I now have a potentially broken toe."

"What?" he says with a laugh. "How did all of that happen?"

"Because I'm Sarah Mason, that's how. What time are we supposed to be there?" I grab a lipstick tube out of my cosmetics case and cradle the phone against my shoulder as I mindlessly swipe it on.

"I told you yesterday, hon. We need to be there at two o'clock. I'm taking an hour off work. Are you okay to grab a cab?"

"I was just going to catch the L." I drop the lipstick and pick up my mascara, rushing through the process and not really concentrating on what I'm doing before dropping it, grabbing my perfume bottle, and spritzing some on.

"You do know you'll be wearing a wedding dress, right? You haven't forgotten that fact?"

I shrug. "It's not like it's a big poufy gown with a long train. It's a formal white dress that just happens to be what I'm getting married in."

"Sez, hon…" Wyatt's voice goes soft. "We don't have to do this if you're having second thoughts."

"We do have to do this, Wyatt, and you know why. I love you like a brother and in…" I pull the phone from my ear to look at the time. "Shit! I'm so freaking late. I'll see you there at two… maybe…"

"Okay."

I giggle, a genuine smile forming on my lips. "Alright, soon-to-be hubby, let me go so I can get dressed and leave."

"See you there."

"I really do appreciate what you're doing for me, Wyatt. I hope you know that?"

"I do. And I really hope *you* know that I would do anything for you. I mean, what's a wedding between besties?"

"Exactly," I reply.

"And Sez?

"Yeah?"

"Don't forget the tiara. If you don't wear it, I swear to God I'll stand you up at the altar. Runaway brides won't have anything on a runaway gay groom."

"But—" I don't get to voice my protest because Wyatt has hung up on me.

Dammit.

Get your copy of Promising Bliss here

OTHER BOOKS BY BJ HARVEY

Romantic Comedy

Bliss Series

Temporary Bliss (Bliss #1)—Mac and Daniel

True Bliss (Bliss #2)—Kate and Zander

Reclaiming Bliss (Bliss #3)—Sean and Sam

formerly Blissful Surrender

Permanent Bliss (Bliss #4)—

Mac & Daniel's Wedding

Finding Bliss (Bliss #5)—Noah and Zoe

Building Bliss (formerly Game Player)—Matt and Mia

Secret Bliss (formerly Game Maker)

—Zack and Danika

Faking Bliss (formerly Game Saver)

—Cade and Abi

Seeking Bliss (formerly Game Ender)

—Thomas and Amy

Promising Bliss (formerly Game Breaker)

—Cameron and Sarah

Beautiful Bliss (formerly Game Planner)

—Jase and Natalie

Cook Brothers Series (Game series spin-off) - House Flipping Rom Coms

Work in Progress — Jamie and April

Work Violation — Jax and Ronnie

Working Back — Bryant and Faith

Hard Work — Cohen and Skye

Working For It — Ezra and Gilly

Chicago First Responders

(Cook Brothers spin-off)

Show Stopper — Marco and Renee

Life Changer — Rhodes and Delilah

Miracle Worker — Gio and Alex

Rule Bender — Luca and London

Holiday Romance

Stranded (Christmas novella with Bliss connection)

Contemporary Romance

Chances Series

One Shot (Chances #1)

Second Chance (Chances #2)

Third Strike (Chances #3)

Sovereign Series

Touch (Sovereign Part One)

Taste (Sovereign Part Two)

Feel (Sovereign Part Three)

Romance Suspense

Lost Series

Lost in Distraction (Lost #1)

Lost For You (Lost #2)

Lost Without You (Lost #3)

Standalone

Crave